THE DEFIANT LADY PENCAVEL,

a satirical Georgian farce

BY

DIANE SCOTT LEWIS

Dedication

to my sons, Christopher and Jeffry

Author's Note

all clichés, redundancies, startling coincidences, and anachronisms

are presented here for fun and on purpose

D0167381

The Defiant Lady Pencavel

by

Diane Scott Lewis

ISBN-13: 978-1492906247
ISBN-10: 1492906247

Electronic version published by:
Books We Love Ltd.
Chestermere, Alberta Canada

http://bookswelove.net

Copyright 2013 by Diane Scott Lewis
Published by Diane H. Parkinson

Cover art by: Michelle Lee Copyright 2013

Chapter One

The coach lurched to a stop on the circular drive, before the impressive Palladian mansion with its strong vertical lines, classical style and large central portico. Lady Melwyn Pencavel released the wrist strap and stared across at her abigail. "Well, here we are, home, to emptiness and routine—and my excruciating death, I daresay. I hope dear Papa won't scold me too severely."

"He most often scolds, m'lady, don't he?" Clowenna gave her the usual smirk born from her years of suffering as Melwyn's partner in misdeed. "Truth be told, 'ee does tend to misbehave, an' on purpose if I do say so."

"What else is there left for a woman to do in this repressive society? You won't ever be forced into an unwanted marriage. I'm nearly one and twenty, and my betrothed is almost forty. He'll be in his dotage soon." Melwyn opened the door, almost hitting the waiting footman in the face. He let down the step. She alighted and breathed in the brisk air, the welcome scents of boxwood and lavender. The March spring blooms were starting, peeling off the greyness of winter. She loved her home, yet more often of late it seemed a prison.

"'Ee hasn't seen the gentleman in question since merely a child in leadin' strings. He may pass muster now." Clowenna climbed down after her, adjusting her shawl and the straw hat over her round face.

"I can only hope he'll die early, and leave me a rich widow—*if* I consent to this misalliance, of which I will do my best not to." Melwyn rearranged the muslin skirt of her pink, flowing, risen-waisted gown. The low neckline would scandalize her father, but it was the fashion. She ascended the marble steps and entered Langoron House.

She removed her cloak and pressed her gloves into the hands of their old retainer, Bastian.

"Welcome home, m'lady. I trust your, ah, impromptu journey to Plymouth was...*un*eventful." He bowed the craggy, solemn face—a requirement for butlers she'd always surmised—that stayed somber. He looked as dried up as a stack of old apples, even as his gaze was as warm as plum pudding.

"Dear Bastian, Plymouth is quite lively when the fleet is in." She gave him a mysterious smile and headed for the stairs. "I danced a jig or two."

"I pray not. However, your honorable father wishes to speak to you, m'lady." Bastian twitched his astute stare toward the library. Did she detect a mischievous glint? "The moment you arrive, he said."

"Very well. I must face the consequences, and listen to never-ending lamentations on my hoydenish ways." She took a deep breath and strode into the library. Why did she have to feel like a naughty little girl called before her governess?

Her father sat behind his wide walnut desk, his melancholy grey eyes roving over her as if searching for splashes of mud or far worse. "So, you've graced us with your presence at last." He steepled his fingers and stared at her over his half-spectacles. "I suppose you did your best to ruin your reputation while gamboling about the coast. I ask myself over and over, where did I go wrong?"

"Never fear, dear Papa. I gamboled in disguise. No one would know I was an earl's daughter." She tried her sweetest smile on him, to no avail. "And I'm still pure and untouched, so you need have no worries there either." She should have slept with a few sailors, or the odd stevedore, before consigning herself like a serving of meat to the boring Lord Lambrick.

Her father sighed, tilting his triangular face topped with the grey hair she was certain she had caused. "If only your mother were alive, you would be a more dutiful child." He tapped the leather blotter on his desk. "Fortunately, you *are* no longer a child, and it is time for you to marry, while the estimable viscount will still have you."

"Perhaps he won't; or he may decide he's too ancient to marry." She twirled about to soften her frustration, and caught her reflection in the window: slender figure with full bosom, honey-blonde hair framing an oval face with pretty, pouty lips that fooled men into thinking her complacent. Any man would be privileged to have her. Yet she didn't wish to give up her freedom. She twisted at the silver cord with two large tassels that was tied around her waist. "Why must I marry at all?"

"My dear, every proper young woman marries. The *ton* notices any dereliction of behavior. Do you wish to be a disgraced spinster, taking care of her father in his declining years? I would be honored with your company, but you are a young lady of restless nature, and need far more guidance than I've managed to supply."

He stood, his mouth in a grimace. His short stature and frail frame were dwarfed by the desk.

She knew she'd inherited her tall, graceful form from her mother—but prayed that was all. A comely visage could attract too much debauchery. Melwyn shivered before collecting herself once more.

"You know I'm devoted to you, Papa...to a point." She sighed; he was correct about her restless nature. "Nevertheless, why should I care what a herd of stale biddies thinks of me just because I won't conform to the dictates of society?" She flipped an errant ringlet from her cheek. "I imagine they are all bored to the teeth themselves, but too stuck in their customs and ruts to crawl out and enjoy life."

"Be that as it may, I've written to his lordship, and he should be here in a few days. Let us opine that he won't find you wanting." He waved a weary hand in dismissal. "Go to your room and scrub Plymouth from your skin. I expect you to pretend to be the perfect lady when Lord Lambrick arrives."

"Oh, fie. If I must. I will only meet with him to please you, Papa." She almost stomped her foot, then thought against it. If she wanted to be taken seriously, she must stop acting the spoiled moppet even when such actions hid her anxieties. Flouncing toward the door, she said, "But I cannot change who I am, a woman of independent spirit." Her heart hammered at the idea she was soon to meet her betrothed—for the first time as a mature young woman.

"Sadly, I blame myself. I've allowed you to run loose like an untamed foal since your mother died when you were only twelve. I should have remarried." Another heavy sigh emanated from him. "And please wear a kerchief with that dress."

Melwyn rushed up the stairs and entered her bedchamber. "Papa is in high dudgeon, though he usually is, the poor dear. He's droning on about Mother again," she said to her abigail.

Clowenna slowly folded Melwyn's clothes into the clothes press. Her steady, stocky form had been an anchor—sometimes a burr—in her life since Melwyn was ten. "La, I does hope 'ee kept quiet on that subject, m'lady?"

"Of course. He lives in his fantasy that Mother is dead. But I've known the truth from the beginning. Mama ran off with the second under-butler." Melwyn sat in her favorite wing-backed chair and tried to relax her taught muscles. "I suppose I get my brazen ways from her, but I'll never forgive her for abandoning me. And why wasn't the *first* under-butler good enough?"

Clowenna straightened and smoothed the plain linen open-robe gown she wore. Her pale hair, the color of straw, pulled up in a bun, made her look like a serving of whipt syllabub. "Did 'ee expect your mam an' her lover to drag a querulous girl about wi' them? That o' spoiled their fun, wouldn't it?"

"You are maddingly correct." Melwyn flung that thought aside. She untied the pink satin ribbon beneath her chin and removed her straw hat covered in rose velvet. The years had softened her ache for a mother in her life. Resentment toward her absent parent had replaced it. Her youth had been filled with nurses and governesses, who usually managed to offer her kind attention if no true affection. "Papa worries *I'll* embarrass him. I'm certain by now the holier-than-everyone *bon ton* has found out about Mother's escapade."

"We is far removed from London here in the west country." Clowenna laid sprigs of lavender in the drawers where she'd placed her lady's chemises and stays. "Let's hope no one's found out there, or they'd cut your father when he went to town."

"He rarely leaves Cornwall. Poor dear Papa, I shouldn't plague him so. But now he's invited my esteemed betrothed here." Melwyn kicked off her slippers. She rubbed her stocking-clad feet together, her upset prickling along her shoulders. "Perhaps I will disappoint Lord Lambrick, and he'll want nothing to do with me."

"I've no doubt you'll encourage his disgust, m'lady." Clowenna, at six years older, gave her best mother hen look of reprimand. "Yet he may be your last chance for a decent life."

"Are you so certain I want a decent, and ultimately dreary, life?" Melwyn unpinned her hair and dragged her fingers through the strands. "Why aren't *my* desires important?"

"Will 'ee ever tell the master your real reason for goin' to Plymouth?"

"To view that rare Greek vase the sea captain brought back?" Melwyn rubbed her fingertips along her scalp. "Papa would never understand my fascination for a red and black painted vessel used for libations from the fifth century B.C."

"Plain cream ware crockery works just as well, don't it?" Clowenna picked up a pitcher and poured water into the ewer.

"I'd much rather be of rare Athenian amphora than simple Bodmin pottery." Melwyn unlaced her bodice. "Ultimately, I'm only worthy as a girl of clean virtue to marry off."

Melwyn sighed. Her memories of Lord Lambrick were hazy. A tall, lean man with striking dark eyes; eyes full of mischief and something a little menacing that might intrigue her, if he hadn't evolved into the tiresome dullard of most of his ilk—and strangled her future in his dubious hands.

****

Griffin Lambrick, the Viscount of Merther, strolled past the kitchen garden where spicy smells reminded him of when he'd romped here as a boy, pulling out plants to irritate cook. The air near the sea remained damp and he prayed for no storms to ruin his plans—though his plans were weeks from now and turbulent flaws could rise at any time.

He'd just left his tenants in the village he provided, giving them extra food from his gardens. When you took good care of your people, they remained loyal and worked hard for you—and aided and abetted when needed.

He entered his two-hundred-year-old Elizabethan manor, passed through the scullery, kitchens, the green baize door, out of the scent of food, and into the "genteel" portion of the house. His late mother would never have even considered setting one dainty toe in the kitchens. Griffin was certain his father would have been scandalized at the very idea. How utterly traditional and unimaginative his parents had been.

Griffin smiled in reminiscence with a dip of sadness—he did miss them and their often distracted, yet benign attention, as a dutiful son should—and entered his library. This room's rich leather smell soothed his restless mind—for a time.

"I was just about to come find 'ee, sir." Jacca, his bailiff, turned from a corner desk.

The Neoclassical piece by Maggiolini had been brought back from Italy by Griffin on his grand tour of the continent. The extensive inlay and marquetry of multiple rare woods over a walnut sub-structure had drawn him, as had a certain Italian beauty.

"What requires my immediate attention?" Griffin paced about the chamber where he'd spent untold hours reading the classics, when he wasn't galloping on his favorite steed over his extensive acres. Or performing the hazardous undertakings that kept his ardor alive.

His chest heated—albeit briefly—at the uncomfortable fact that his parents would have been disappointed in him.

"Sir?" Jacca—with his long, glum face lined by well over forty years—had led Merther Manor since

Griffin was a lad. The bailiff stepped fully into the light from a window, and continued, "A letter has—"

"Where did you get that bruised eye?" Griffin asked, taken aback by the purple discoloring around his bailiff's right eye. "Bear baiting again? Betting at cock fights? Falling down drunk at the local kiddley?"

"'Tis nothing, sir." Jacca shrugged and lowered his head. "Me missus planted me a facer for bein' late for supper. An' I was only five minutes tardy. But nothin' pleases her no more."

"You should really do something about that woman. The laws say you can correct your wife, but nothing about her correcting you," Griffin admonished. Females should be kept firmly in their place or they tended to spiral out of control—though meek girls bored him, he must admit. That temperamental Italian mistress had kept his interests for nearly two years, then she'd demanded marriage. Aware he couldn't wed such a lower-class woman, they'd parted amicably enough after monetary compensation. He'd never loved her. He doubted he was capable of such an emotion, except when it came to his family.

"What I was about to say is, a missive arrived for 'ee." Jacca held out a sealed letter. "Looks important, it does."

"How are my affairs? Soon I'll be off to London to consult with my man of business and I want to be aware of any details I should be apprised of. Have the deplorable estate taxes risen again?" Griffin took the letter without glancing at it.

"Naw, sir." His bailiff flipped open an account book. "An' everythin' runs smoothly at your properties, as always. The sheep produce well, the wool good an' selling in West Riding at them new manufactories."

"Ah, the manufactories. They're putting the cottage industries out of business, people out of work and on parish relief." Griffin leaned against his large desk, unbuttoned his frock coat, and slapped the ignored letter across his knee. "And the aristocracy, such as I, fund the parish relief, which is the least we can do." He tapped the letter, still not looking at it. "I encourage progress, but it hurts the common people."

"Ess, it does. As far as smooth running of affairs, our nocturnal dealin's be an entire different matter." Jacca winked his un-bruised eye, but it barely stirred his craggy features.

"My man of business is well-acquainted with our secret transactions, as you well know." Griffin warmed at the idea of the risks he took. Danger kept life exhilarating. A reason to rise from bed each morning, especially now that the house was lonelier after his mother and father's unfortunate accident at the manor chapel when an embossed ceiling beam had fallen on them during prayer three years past—and his younger brother's death in the Austrian Netherlands the year before that. Griffin stiffened against the carved edge of the desk. He hated to dwell on such losses.

He sighed and glanced at the letter's seal. A fancifully executed P was pressed into the red wax. He fought down a grimace.

Jacca watched him carefully. "You look a bit pale, if I may be so bold. Bad news?"

"I'm anticipating unwelcome, *or* if I could be hopeful, a refusal from this party on something agreed to many years ago." Griffin broke the seal and read. His stomach sank as if he'd swallowed a lead ball. He'd put this arrangement into the recesses of his memory, and now it stared him in the face like a pregnant tavern wench accusing him of paternity. "Deuce it all. The Earl Pencavel is forcing my hand."

Chapter Two

Melwyn twirled in the middle of the spread-out circle of stones that thrust up like granite sentries from the heather on the Bodmin Moor. "I wish I had magic powers and could fly off to Greece, or rather first to Italy, free from distasteful contracts made when I was too young to protest."

A curlew flapped overhead as if mocking her in flight.

"We all has our duties to bear, don't we? Me more an' 'ee." Clowenna stood off to the side, the wind off the moor tugging at her scarf. "'Tis a mite cold out here, m'lady, an' my gloves be not as warm an' fine as yours."

"I'll buy you new gloves at Michaelmas. Don't servants, or most uneducated people, believe in the power of the stones?" Melwyn teased with a wry grin. She scrutinized a nearby quoit, six supporting stones with a capstone that formed an internal chamber. "This was built in the early Neolithic period, about 3500 BC, and it's thought it was originally covered by a mound."

"Looks like a pile o' rubble to me." The maid hunched in her spenser jacket. "Learned or no, some ancient fools had too much time on their hands."

Melwyn inhaled the damp air and held her cloak close. "But we're Cornish. This is part of our heritage. I was always fascinated by the megalithic long cairns and these stone circles." At first, she'd used such interests to ignore the deterioration of her parents' marriage—

her mother's neglect of her—then a burning concentration took over.

"Then why Italy? Why not dig about here in our homeland?"

"I want to broaden my horizons, if I can evade my abysmal *intended*." Melwyn surveyed the standing stones to redirect her thoughts. "The Hurlers are supposed to be a group of men frozen in stone by St. Cleer for playing sports on the Lord's day." She'd climbed them as a girl, now she studied their mystery. Who had placed them here and why? She pointed at two isolated, tall thin stones. "Those are called the Pipers."

"I see no pipes, nor lips to play 'em." Clowenna rubbed her upper arms. "Don't 'ee quality hate superstition?"

"Alas, we do." Melwyn's shoulders sagged. "We're supposed to lead by example. But I need moments of mirth. Lord Lambrick could be here any day to devour me." She shivered, from that inevitability and the cold breeze. "Why are men allowed to remain unmarried, roam and cavort, but women are not?" She faced the weak sun. "I'm hoping to burn my face, acquire freckles, so the viscount will be repulsed by me."

"Too early in the year for that, m'lady." Clowenna wrapped her scarf close. "An' blather on at the poor sod, that should do it."

"You're right, my shrew of an abigail, and I mean that in the kindest way." Melwyn laughed, chasing her qualms like marbles about inside her. "After all, I can refuse him since the indenture was made while I was underage. I just hate to disappoint Papa yet again." If only she had a wise mother to turn to for advice. However, *her* mother would have encouraged her to shag a servant.

That distant twinge of regret wriggled through her.

A footman dressed in the silver and blue embroidered coat and knee-breeches of the Pencavel livery ran over the heather in their direction. He doffed his bicorn hat. "Your father has had word. The viscount should be here by tomorrow, my lady."

Melwyn swayed then hardened with affront. "I will face him without fear, and disappoint him from the moment we meet."

"Oh, la. I have no doubt o' that. I could use a cup o' tea." Clowenna groaned and turned toward home. "What if he be a nice gent, what then?"

Melwyn took a deep breath as she stepped along the rocky ground where the first sprigs of meadow sweet sprang up. "Then he will be deterred all the more faster." She prayed he wouldn't be too nice; even her relentless determination should have its limits.

****

Clowenna jerked the laces of Melwyn's stays tighter. She exhaled in a whoosh as the whale bones dug into her flesh through her cotton chemise. "Ooof. I feel like a sausage. I've heard that in France they've stopped wearing corsets or any undergarments."

"And they're also lopping heads from bodies, so we shouldn't follow none o' their choices." Clowenna tied the laces. She helped Melwyn slip on her claret-colored gown with fringed stomacher. "This be a bold hue for a late afternoon, m'lady."

"I wish to impress Lord Lambrick with my, let's say, fiery persona." Melwyn laughed, though inside she dreaded this meeting. Her stomach knotted. "He's come here to peer at the horrid mistake he's made, being the son of father's close friend, and probably agreeing to this union three sheets to the wind after several glasses of port."

"Try not to be too offensive. Show your father what fine breedin' 'ee has." Her abigail pulled the hot curling iron from the flames in the fireplace and primped at her mistress's chignon. "Or should o' had."

"An example of the usual schooling, embroidery, painting, pianoforte, and oh, the fact her mother is living in sin with a servant? That sort of breeding, do you mean?" Melwyn preened in the cheval mirror; she did cut a fine figure. Her bosom swelled from the bodice like two creamy orbs. "We women are taught to be useful but not too intelligent."

"'Tis true. But please gentle your words in his lordship's company." Clowenna wrapped a white silk handkerchief around Melwyn's throat. "This will make 'ee look a mite pure an' hide your bubbies."

"If I'm to impress him as a future wife, shouldn't I show off my womanly charms?" Melwyn removed the silk and tossed it on her bed. "Or he'll think I'm a wanton of the first order and scuttle away."

"Don't scandalize him with no talk o' diggin' for relics, m'lady." Clowenna refolded the scarf, shaking her head in resignation.

"Why must women have to pretend to be simple-minded to please men? I'm proud of my expertise in the romance languages, which will help me on the continent." It chafed her to be in "polite" society. Talks of fashion (well, she did enjoy fashion now and then), the Prince of Wales' disastrous marriage to Caroline of Brunswick, or tittering over a man's silly jokes, irked her. Anything with boundaries felt suffocating. Is that how her mother had felt?

Melwyn left her room and hesitated at the top of the staircase. She trembled in anticipation. Lord Lambrick had arrived last night, after she'd retired. Now she'd come face to face with this man who years earlier hadn't seemed such a threat to her happiness.

Her father stood in the hall with a tall stranger. The gilt bronze chandelier above them flickered with many candles.

"And here is my lovely, so gently bred, daughter." Her father turned, his gaze hopeful on that issue, along with the slim man beside him.

Gliding down the stairs, she took stock of their guest. He had dark brows and the striking eyes she'd remembered. His black hair was tied back in a queue, his face lean and handsome—though he reminded her of someone you wouldn't care to meet alone on a remote path.

He made a slight, almost mocking, bow as he assessed her. His tailored buff frockcoat and breeches fit him like a glove. He showed well-built legs in white silk stockings, his buckled shoes polished.

"Lord Lambrick, may I present my daughter, Lady Melwyn Pencavel."

Melwyn gave a shallow curtsy. He didn't look impressed and that annoyed her, while also giving her hope he'd refute her. "I suppose I'm honored to meet you, sir."

"As am I to see you again, my lady." His deep voice sounded cold, which caught her off-balance. Still, this was what she'd prayed for. "Griffin Lambrick, at your service. It has been a long while since we've met."

"An Incredibly long and unpredictable time, I'd imagine." She gave him a fleeting smile. "Things change, people change, don't you agree?"

"Good manners should never change. Shall we have refreshment in the parlor?" Father ushered them into that room with its ornate plaster ceiling, upholstered furniture and small walnut tables—a neglected place where ladies once sipped tea. He poured them glasses of sherry.

"How have you busied yourself all this time, my lord?" Melwyn sipped the sweet beverage. "During all these years you've never bothered to revisit here? Not that I minded in the least." Yet she might have discouraged him that much sooner.

"A bold question, is it not?" He looked amused, for an instant. He had a few lines around his eyes and on his brow, his skin sun-burnished. No pasty-faced man of quality was he. "I have numerous interests, and estates to manage."

"Do you not pay someone to manage them for you?" She gave him a wide-eyed look of innocence. However, his close contemplation unnerved her, and she disliked the feeling. "Certainly you'd never tax your own exertions."

"Melwyn, my dear," Father cautioned. "If you will please refrain from such–"

"Sorry, Papa, but talk of niceties tires me." She wished she could dissemble, after seeing her parent's sad expression. She fingered the intricate grooves in her crystal glass. "We might discuss Dr. Jenner's recent discovery, the small pox vaccination."

"Ah, a well-read girl, how refreshing." Lambrick's tone was satirical. "And what do you do, other than hone your rapier tongue, to busy yourself, my lady?"

She was relieved Lambrick didn't fawn over her, or make false compliments. "I ride, read, travel when I can. Soon, I intend to visit the excavations in Pompeii, Italy."

"That is out of the question, my dear," her father groaned. "Ladies do not make such excursions, unless with family or a *husband*."

"What do you know about excavations, Miss Pencavel?" Lambrick narrowed his eyes.

"I also follow the events across the channel. The bloody Terror, as it was called, two years past, in 1794." She was taken aback by his sharp inquiry, and decided to change the subject.

Her father's eyes widened further in dismay. He pulled his Bilston enamel snuffbox from his waistcoat pocket. "Uh hem, as you can see, Lord Lambrick, my daughter is familiar with the news *and* the latest classical fashion from France, although she seems to have dressed for the opera tonight. Let us hope that is all those frog-eaters import. They should never have murdered their king in the name of republicanism."

"They murdered the king because he tried to escape, and incriminating letters to his wife's Austrian relatives were found in his possession." She paced toward the ornate, marble hearth, certain Lambrick would board the first coach out of the district now.

"You are well informed, my lady. Perhaps too much so." Lambrick's eyes twinkled. Had she made a mistake and impressed him?

"My beautiful daughter is really quite adept at...was it cooking, no, sewing, doubtful...?" Her father scratched his head in quandary.

"I'm capable at anything I wish, and far from being a silly schoolgirl." She turned, fringe swinging, and stared at the faded rectangle on the wall where her mother's portrait used to hang. Father had finally removed it last year. She blew out her breath "I can learn as well as any man."

"I may have allowed her too much access to the lending library." Papa fumbled with the snuffbox lid painted with a bucolic setting. "How are affairs at your estate here in Cornwall, your lordship?" He took a pinch of snuff. "Merther Manor, near Padstow? A grand place I once visited often, where *any* woman would be proud to preside over."

"We're busy with our sheep; wool is productive to clothe the soldiers fighting for His Majesty on the continent, against the rabble, ruthless French." Lambrick appeared to wince when he said "French," surprising her.

"And to bury our dead, since a previous king decreed it to promote our wool industry." Melwyn set down her glass, her smile challenging. Then she had difficulty meeting the viscount's dark gaze, and didn't know why. "You must be extremely wealthy and able to pluck a bride from any of the major families you might choose."

"Egad, I should have married the Widow Whale. She'd have been a calming influence," Father muttered to himself. He dropped his snuffbox in his pocket. "Please *try* to remember your deportment, my dear. I...I will consult our housekeeper to see if dinner is ready." He lumbered from the room like a beleaguered, beaten dog.

"Forgive me, Papa." Her heart began to sink, but she must remain strong.

"I take it you have no interest in being mistress of Merther Manor?" Lambrick arched a sardonic eyebrow.

"I only wanted you to know what sort of bargain you'd struck, so there will be no misconceptions, if I agree to go through with this." She walked toward him, trying not to notice his patrician profile. An aura exuded from him she couldn't define, like the moment before a storm. "I'm not some timid female who will swoon over your every word."

"Is it myself who offends you, my lady, or men in general?" He smiled slowly, which rendered him more handsome.

"Oh, men are fine when they're not arrogant, and I know little about you. It's husbands I don't trust." She forced herself to meet his gaze steadily. "Or the idea of a husband, you might say."

His eyes traveled across her, and up her, halting at her low bodice with a cold calculating expression.

"You have a strange manner of dress if you hope to discourage any man."

"Well, stop eyeing me like a prize ewe. If you want a stupid, compliant wife, you need to look elsewhere." She fought a prickle at his scrutiny.

"If you stop heaving your bosom at me, I might find it easier to look elsewhere." He smirked and finished his drink.

Her cheeks heated; but what had she expected? She tugged up her neckline. The viscount's boorish behavior made this so much easier. "Then I assume you will tell my father that we don't suit at all?"

"Unfortunately, I'm beginning to think we might suit, as I detest simpering females." He poured himself another sherry. "Indeed, the idea of you *is* a daunting prospect. And women do require a taut harness."

She seethed inside. He continued to mock her. "I believe you are too old for me, sir, and will never keep up. Don't suppose you will ever suppress me."

"That remains to be seen, my dear. I am all of two and thirty, so still quite robust." He raised his glass. "I came here with the intention of informing your father that I desire no flibbertigibbet slip of a girl, especially one whose mother cannot restrain herself from flipping up her skirts for a lackey."

"How *dare* you." Melwyn felt punched in the stomach, even as she admired his candor. She gripped her hand on the back of the triple-arched sofa upholstered in striped silk. "You are a jackanapes, sir. I will never marry you."

"Truthfully, you will find few who will dare, my lovely earl's daughter, after your peccadilloes about the region." He chuckled, chucked her under the chin, turned and departed the chamber.

Melwyn rushed to the hearth and smacked her hand on the marble mantel. Her skin smarted, and the ormolu clock and two gold candlesticks jostled. She glared again at the faded rectangle on the wallpaper. "Double fie! What will I do now? I cannot allow him to best me, and I'll *never* marry such a blackguard—or any man!"

Chapter Three

Griffin held tight to his horse's reins. Why did he always taunt fate? He should have simply written to Earl Pencavel and asked to have the betrothal rescinded. Something integral in his nature drove him to act the devil-may-care. Perhaps he'd been hit too hard by a cricket bat at Harrow.

He twisted at the leather. Then when his brother Alan was commissioned into the army, and the devastating results, Griffin's reckless attitude increased. Life could be over in such short order.

Now the arousing figure and derisive tone of Miss Pencavel disrupted his composure. He gritted his teeth. He'd left Langoron House as soon as he'd informed the earl he had to think the situation over.

Rain started to splatter on his face. The dots of moisture were cold comfort. He trotted his mount into the yard of Jamaica Inn and an ostler rushed out.

An isolated place high on the Bodmin Moor, the L-shaped, two-storied inn was a notorious hideout for smugglers to conceal their contraband on its way up country. Griffin was familiar with its operations. Tea, silks, tobacco and brandy had been smuggled through Cornwall since customs dues were first introduced in the thirteenth century.

The government kept enacting laws to stop it, but many the revenuer would accept the odd bribe. Griffin had the misfortune of attracting the few honest excise men left—but that only added to the intrigue.

Inside the expansive taproom with low, thick beams, he ordered a brandy and sat near the granite hearth. Smoke and the smell of alcohol drifted around him. He could break the betrothal, or allow Miss Pencavel to do so, if he revealed his bad character. She was not yet in her majority, so would be perfectly in her right to rebuff him. They'd spent no private time together, so he couldn't be accused of impropriety with her, as tempting a piece as she was.

She didn't seem concerned that her reputation might be tarnished by putting an end to the agreement. In fact, she acted too anxious to dissolve their arrangement.

He fought a smile as he'd always savored a challenge.

Griffin took a long drink from his glass, the smooth taste warming him. Miss Pencavel was beautiful, and captivating, if you enjoyed being berated. But he had no need for such a creature. He was reluctant to take on a wife at all. Then why prolong this farce?

He only worried that the earl might threaten a breach-of-promise suit at a final refusal, though the man appeared to be of mild character. His father had often said his friend Pencavel should have more back-bone, especially when it came to his feckless wife. Hopefully—for *her* sake of course—the daughter didn't harbor the same base inclinations.

A grizzled man approached. He wore worn linen breaches, along with the leather gaiters sported by the working class. "Lord Lambrick, is it?"

Griffin glanced up into the stranger's dirty face. He'd made arrangements to meet someone here, but had to be careful. "I could be. Who wants to know?"

"Name's Clem, sir. Might I sit?" The man sat before being invited. He leaned a grubby sleeve over the table. "I been told 'ee be the man to speak to, by a mutual friend."

"I have few friends. And you are too brash, and unwashed, for your own good." Griffin sipped more of his brandy to hide his suspicion. The embers in the blackened hearth sizzled and snapped. "You wish to speak to me about what, specifically?"

"I might have somethin' downstairs 'ee should be interested in." Clem's foul breath blew across the table.

Laughter from a group of miners in soiled drill coats soared from another table. A buxom girl sashayed by with pewter tankards of ale. Her ample cleavage almost made up for her pock-marked face.

"Are you here to trap me into something nefarious, my uncouth fellow?" Griffin asked in mock severity even as his curiosity rose. "My revenge would be painful."

"Don't worry none, sir. I'm as honest as a man can be, an' still be a criminal." Clem chuckled coolly. "I heard you be wooin' the earl's pretty daughter. A ripe handful she be, ess?"

"That is none of your business. I'd watch my tongue if I were you." Griffin's defense of Lady Pencavel was stronger than he intended. He gripped his brandy glass, already anxious to be done with this fetid fellow.

"No disrespect, beg pardon." The man tugged on his forelock, yet his gaze remained sly. "Come wi' me, sir, an' I'll show 'ee what I have. That's what you're here for, true?"

"You're assuming much...and yes. But what you have may hold no interest for me at all as I am a cultured and discerning man." Griffin didn't trust this scavenger, but he'd dealt with many the low character before. He'd have to give their "mutual friend" a good dressing down if this was a mistake. "I insist you provide me with more details."

"These items...they be like the guineas an' shillings we has here, but from backalong times in Italy." Clem snickered and beamed as if he'd offered the crown jewels.

"Very well, it might be worth a look. But I warn you, no tomfoolery. I am not a man to cross. Or run afoul of, or broadside, and so on." Griffin nodded and rose slowly to his feet. He felt the cool brass handle of the pistol in his coat pocket, leery of footpads, swindlers and cut-purses.

****

The billowing smoke of London almost choked her, and Melwyn closed the coach window in irritation. "I haven't visited here in a couple of years, and had forgotten what a beastly stink this city is. The kennels are teaming with offal."

The coach rumbled over the raised pedestrian walkways, past brick, and wattle and daub buildings that leaned like drunks over a table—the few such structures left after the Great Fire of 1666. The numerous shop signs, which no longer dangled over people's heads as a few had fallen and killed the passersby, fascinated Melwyn, and softened her pique at having to flee Cornwall.

"How did 'ee snatch the coach and horses, again, without your father's knowin'?" Clowenna pressed a handkerchief to her nose.

"I have my wiles. Anything to slip away from that vile Lord Lambrick." She shivered in revulsion, yet his mesmerizing eyes haunted her dreams. "He'll never have me to wed and bed. Whatever that might mean, since I'm a virgin and wouldn't know."

"But why London, m'lady? After five days o' travel at indifferent inns?" Clowenna brushed soot from the shoulders of her spencer jacket, then rubbed her tailbone. "Me bum is numb."

"To hide with my windowed aunt, of course. Doesn't everyone have a widowed aunt tucked away in London for convenience?" Melwyn tugged her pelisse close. "For people of my class, it is *de rigueur*."

At Grosvenor Square, in the exclusive Mayfair district, the two women alighted. The pale-stoned townhomes with Corinthian columns and several stories lorded over the park before them. Elegant carriages clattered over the cobblestones.

"Your father will know where we is." Clowenna stepped around steaming horse dung. "Your aunt bein' his sister."

"I'll be of age in six months, and then he can't force me to do anything." Melwyn regretted she sounded like a child with that statement as she smoothed her wrinkled skirt.

"Six months be a long time, m'lady. What choices does 'ee have, if not to marry?"

"I'll marry a footman, if needs must, then run off before the fateful bedding, disguise myself as a man and join the navy and travel to the ruins in Italy and Greece." Melwyn shoved aside her ire that her maid was correct in her assumption about choices, and approached the intricately carved door.

"Will be flogged in the navy, given your temper," Clowenna said thoughtfully.

Melwyn laughed, for the first time in a week. She stared again at the door. She hadn't seen her aunt for two years, and hoped she'd be welcomed. Hesitating, she turned to her abigail. "I still wonder how that brigand Lambrick knew about Mama."

"We should o' stayed in Cornwall an' asked him." Clowenna flicked a smut from her eyelashes. "An' I doubt someone with your pride would marry a footman."

"What do you mean, my pride? If I had any pride, I'd sit home and knit, smile blandly at all men, and sink into despair." Melwyn jerked the bell pull. "Really, Clowenna, you have the bellicose manner of a virago. I don't know why I keep you with me."

"Because no one else puts up with 'ee, m'lady?" Clowenna rolled her eyes. "An' if 'ee wasn't so fair to look at, you'd never get away wi' your mischief."

The front door creaked open and the typical stiff-lipped butler stared down his long nose at them.

"Please inform her ladyship that her niece is here and seeks sequestering." Melwyn walked past him as if he were invisible, as certain servants should be.

"Very good, m'lady." The man shut the door, almost closing it on Clowenna.

Melwyn smelled the overstuffed rooms and noticed her aunt's old-fashioned decor hadn't changed since her last visit. The rococo still garnished everything like icing on a wedding cake.

"Who is here? I'm not at home to callers today. Who would be so rude as to break that rule?" an imperious voice asked. A woman with a voluptuous figure sauntered down the corridor. Her little lace cap sat atop a mountain of brown hair, like a snow cap on Mt. Everest. Her lilac-colored gown clung to her generous curves. She raised a quizzing glass. "Oh, dear, is that you Melwyn?"

"It is I, dear Auntie Hedra." Melwyn rushed forward and kissed the air on each side of her aunt's papery but still lovely face. The woman smelled like rose water, and a hint of Canary wine. "Can you hide me for a few months, six to be precise?"

"What have you done now, gel?" Her aunt arched a mouse-skin covered eyebrow. "Are you still the hoyden that my poor, delusional brother has never managed to curtail?"

"I am guilty as charged, Auntie." Melwyn removed her pelisse and dropped it in the butler's hands. "I've tried and tried not to vex Papa, but I just can't squeeze myself into the paper-doll conformity that is expected. And *why* is it expected? Don't women have brains the same as men?"

"We do, m'lady, but should use them quiet-like...the power behind the throne, an' all that." Clowenna stepped forward, still rubbing her butt.

"And did you travel all the way to London with no companion, only this person of questionable birth and actions that I see before me?" Aunt Hedra sneered. "This creature stares at me and not at her feet as she ought to."

Melwyn winced. She thought of her maid as an older sister, though would never admit that to her, thus giving her a bigger head then she already had. "You've met Clowenna before; she's been with me for over a decade. I agree that she has the mouth of a fishwife sometimes, but we are inseparable. She's my trusted abigail."

"Hmmm, I see my brother's household is still in pandemonium. Why are you here, and in need of hiding? Aren't you to wed Lord Lambrick?" Aunt Hedra's lips quirked. "He might put a knot in your proverbial tail."

"*That* gentleman, and I use the term loosely, is why I'm here. I don't wish to marry him, ever. He is contemptible, and not in the least intimidated by me." Melwyn fought a quiver.

"High praise, indeed. He is a man of mysterious, even dangerous, repute." Aunt Hedra walked with her up the grand, sweeping staircase designed by Adam. "But you're right; we do want husbands that we can manipulate successfully. My late husband, Lord Penpol, was an indulgent man, with a kind heart. I managed to tread on his every nerve. Cut his life short, I daresay."

She stopped, her mouth in a frown. "I do miss him, oddly enough."

"No one will tell me, but why *must* I marry? Men can go their entire lives and never marry, why not women?" Melwyn huffed, even as the idea that the viscount had a dangerous repute piqued her interest. "Why are we unattached women treated as spinsters who must be hidden away and pitied?"

"Only the quality be expected to marry. Me, I was sold into service, an' hard toil, like a plow ox." Clowenna sighed.

"Some of those unmarried males are whispered about as fowls of a different feather...but I digress." Aunt Hedra's cheeks reddened a shade. "As for we women, we are deemed to have weak minds, and willful natures that must be tamed. You do fit the willful nature portion."

"I think men fear us, that's why they make all these regulations to keep us downtrodden." The familiar frustration pricked along her neck.

"You do have a point, little minx." Aunt Hedra opened a door on the left. Her grey eyes reminded Melwyn of her papa—but her aunt's gaze was far from melancholy. "You may occupy this room, my dear, but don't be surprised if my brother seeks you out here."

"I told her the same," Clowenna muttered. "But would she listen?"

"Your gel does remind me of a fishwife." Aunt Hedra sniffed, studying the maid with her quizzing glass. "Well, put on your finest gown, Mellie. Tonight I've been invited to Vauxhall, and you may go with me, but the abigail stays here."

"I'd love to visit the famous pleasure garden." Melwyn clapped her hands together, chasing aside her guilt at deserting her father when he thought he was doing what was best for her. "Purely for observational reasons."

"Oh, la, there goes them gardens." Clowenna moaned and shuffled into the guest room.

****

The sun hung low over the Thames and painted the tops of the elm and sycamore trees in orange light.

"If Papa shows up in town, which I doubt, can you pretend you never saw me?" Melwyn said as they left the boat at the Vauxhall Stairs, paid their one shilling apiece for admission and walked into the cool Grove of the pleasure garden.

"My sweet niece, we will meet several of my dearest friends here." Aunt Hedra hurried down the path, petticoats rustling. A footman followed behind, carrying her fan. "How will I introduce you, if you wish to keep up this charade of hiding from my cully of a brother?"

"Papa isn't a coward, Auntie. He's only so meek tempered to not be very dynamic." Melwyn bristled at the insult to her parent. She adjusted the over-tunic of her embroidered gown, the turquoise color glistening in the sunlight.

"Your mother found him not very dynamic, I dare swear, or she wouldn't have absconded with the under-butler." Her aunt nodded sagaciously. "Not that I could ever approve of such depraved actions."

"The *second* under-butler," Melwyn corrected. She remembered her mother calling her papa weak-minded, and Melwyn had risen to his defense by throwing a shoe in her nursery. She increased her pace. "Now, you promised me you had a scientist friend from the Royal Society who is supposed to be here. I wish to discuss the ongoing discoveries in Pompeii and Herculaneum with him."

"Ah, the Roman ruins in Italy? Why are you interested in them?" Aunt Hedra steered her down another path called the Grand Walk, past the golden statue of Aurora. The piney and earthy scents of the thick foliage tickled Melwyn's nose.

"I intend to become an archeologist. Digging in the dirt, unearthing fascinating antiquities. Learning how people lived in the past." Melwyn preened. "It is a far better prospect than being buried alive on some gloomy estate while a husband carouses in cheap taverns."

"You will be the death of me and your father." Aunt Hedra sighed. "I suppose you wish to sail off to Egypt and examine one of those pointy objects they build there?"

"The pyramids, I can hardly wait. Hopefully the French won't go there first, then Admiral Nelson will follow, and the Battle of the Nile will take place." Melwyn's heart soared. She imagined herself in a flowing white dress, sitting atop a camel. "But then they'll discover the Rosetta Stone, or perchance *I* will."

"Such foolish tales infect your unfathomable brain. Leave any Rosé stones in the desert with the heathens." Aunt Hedra dragged her along, past piazzas framed by shrubbery, and exclusive supper boxes for private parties. "Look, there is my dear friend, the Duchess of Dumfort. I'll introduce you. Her husband, the duke, resides in Bath most of the year, for his health, so he says."

Framed in the glow of the last rays of sun, a short, wide woman grinned at Aunt Hedra as they approached. Her ostrich feather, stuck in a chignon of silver hair, wavered in the cool breeze. "Hedra, a glorious good evening. The splendor of fresh air. Who is this exquisite young woman with you?"

"My niece, Melwyn Pencavel. She is up from Cornwall for a visit, Your Grace." Aunt Hedra pressed both of Melwyn's shoulders. "Her father is my cherished brother."

"Melwyn? Hedra? You Cornish have such curious names, you'd think you were part of another country." Duchess Dumfort sallied forth in her wide-skirted gown like a green galleon. "How nice to meet you, my child."

"We Cornish are an unusual strain." Melwyn curtsied, recalling a fraction of her deportment training. "I'm certain I'm honored to meet you as well, Your Grace." The woman looked like centuries of good breeding, perhaps a little in-breeding.

"Of course you are, on both counts." The duchess took her arm in her plump, be-ringed, fingers. "Such a lovely child; have you been presented at a season yet?"

"Indeed she has, three seasons ago, then the one after that," Aunt Hedra said. "The young men were all in a flurry over her."

But her outspoken ways had dismayed any beaux, Melwyn mused. "I was betrothed at the time, as I have been for many years, to the unsuitable Lord Lambrick."

"Griffin Lambrick? The Viscount of Merther?" The duchess's eyes flashed. "I've not seen him in London at any social event for many a year." She leaned close to Hedra and whispered, "a bit of a rogue, isn't he? The child would be no match for him. He is very much unsuitable, I agree."

"Alas, she is all of twenty now, and needs to be settled, soon." Aunt Hedra shook her head gravely as if Melwyn had some noxious disease.

"Or I'll wilt on a shelf," Melwyn announced with irony. "And I believe his roguish lordship is no match for *me*, yet I'll never find out, because I've refused him."

"With your father's permission, of course?" The duchess gave her a simpering smile.

A group of jugglers sauntered by, followed by laughing patrons.

"No, with my own permission, your grace. I told him I'd never marry him, and that was that." Melwyn fisted her hands, then flexed out her fingers, deciding that was juvenile. "I never consulted my father, and then I left for London."

"Upon my word." The duchess blanched. "What sort of impudent behavior is this? You will be damaged goods, my dear. You cannot forsake a proposal on your own. Your father must find a good enough reason to refuse a peer. There are ramifications, child." She spoke as if imparting news about an impending French invasion.

"I've warned her about this, your grace. I thought I'd show her the gardens tonight, then send her packing back to Cornwall when she's rested, to either accept the betrothal or have my brother find an appropriate reason to refuse." Aunt Hedra snatched her fan from the footman and fanned herself quickly, tousling her few loose tendrils of hair.

Nightingales warbled from the overhead tree branches.

"I am aware that Lord Lambrick has many sinister rumors about him, so a reason should be easily found." The duchess nodded, as if satisfied with this outcome.

"What are these sinister rumors, pray?" Melwyn stiffened, ready for battle; no one would send her packing. She needed more ammunition, or a passport.

"Nothing fitting for your young, innocent ears." The dumpy duchess glanced around. "Shall we partake of some ice cream? The French, now and then, do create something interesting, other than a machine that chops off heads. Such savagery."

"I'm in agreement for the ice cream, and then we can look for Auntie's friend from the Royal Society." Melwyn walked beside the duchess, whose voluminous skirts almost tripped her. They passed the huge Rotunda, where inside concerts were held. "But I read the Arabs invented ice cream ages ago, then Marco Polo brought it to Europe from China."

"Oh, my dear, stop reading so much, or you will never make a catch of consequence." The duchess patted Melwyn's hand. "You are too pretty to waste your time on books."

"Do *not* mention your mother, we must keep up appearances," Aunt Hedra whispered from behind her fan. "Your grace," she said aloud, "you might know some fascinating and eligible young men to introduce my niece to?"

"I am in no hurry to marry, Auntie, as you well know," Melwyn said through tightening lips. "Where is your friend so we can discuss antiquities? And excuse me for saying, your grace, but reading for knowledge shouldn't be discouraged in young ladies. Many of us don't wish for brains that turn to mush from disuse."

"You will manage your household and a team of rudely unreliable servants, so don't talk such foolishness," the duchess prattled. "A girl without a husband is like a ship without an udder."

Melwyn stifled a laugh. This highly placed peer obviously couldn't tell a boat from a cow.

At the ice cream pavilion, ice packed in straw held pewter bowls of the creamy dessert in various fruit flavors. Melwyn chose raspberry, and wandered to the perimeter of the fading light, half in the shadow to enjoy her treat and calculate her next move. She hated to return to her father if he continued to insist on this marriage. And she wasn't certain of the viscount's feelings after his parting comment in their parlor. She'd repudiated the match, but without her father's permission, as she'd told the duchess. Shame would be brought upon her family, and that was the difficult part. Enough humiliation had been heaped on her papa.

Music drifted over the air, and laughter from the visitors punctuated the antics on the various outdoor stages. The creamy smoothness of the ice cream caressed her taste buds with the tart tang of fruit.

Strong fingers grasped her arm and jerked her into the darkness of high, prickly bushes.

Chapter Four

The chit's wrist felt sparrow-thin in his hands. Griffin glared down at her, as she stared up, raspberry ice cream on her lips. At first startled, she didn't scream and composed herself quickly; he had to admire that.

"How is your sojourn in London, my lady? A sudden urge to travel, had you?" Griffin smiled at the rising anger in her blue eyes.

"How dare you follow me, sir. And drag me into bushes." Miss Pencavel pulled away from him, chin jutted out. "I told you my wishes in Cornwall. You have wasted your time if you're here to change my mind."

"Truth is, I did have business in town, so it's not a total waste." He rocked back on his heels, arms now behind his back. His actions were irrational, and totally alien to his usual demeanor. "You intrigue me, Miss Pencavel, such as a wasp might intrigue one. You wonder how close you may hover before being stung."

He baited her, and enjoyed it. This slip of a girl provoked him, and that was disconcerting. Most females he understood as connivers or simpletons. Miss Pencavel appeared to be neither. Her eyes shone with an innate intelligence. Why *had* he followed her into the garden—while he had to admit that he'd searched for any sign of her in town—when he had little use for marriage? A wife like her would only get in his way.

"I assure you, you will feel my sting." She backed up a step and took another bite of her dessert.

"You said cruel things about my mother. Even if they were true, you were still despicable."

"I must apologize; I should have waited until I knew you better before being so straightforward." He softened his words as a twig crackled under his buckled shoe. "But are you like your mother, partial to servants and other low-lifes?"

"I might be partial to whoever takes my fancy, a sailor, a groom, a particularly handsome nightsoil man." She scrutinized him closely. "I've heard you have sinister inclinations, not that such things would bother me, being the free-thinking person I am, but I'd rather not be troubled with you."

Griffin pondered what she really knew. He decided to deride her, to nudge her off-balance. He resisted the urge to brush a stray leaf from her cheek. "Are you already ruined, my girl, is that why you shy away?"

"I have been in various positions where I might have been ruined, but not in that compromising position I know nothing about, and *you* no doubt insinuate." She licked her spoon, slowly.

Music skirled through the foliage; conversations and laughter ebbed and flowed on the evening air.

Griffin laughed, to allay his increasing attraction to her. Deuce it all; if he wanted a woman he'd pick up a busty tavern wench for a quick roll on the ticking, or other places. His chest tightened. He did not want to desire this little shrew. "You talk a good show, but I think you hide a fearful heart."

Now she laughed. "Fearful of what? Of a man with your reputation? Since I never plan to marry you, I could care less who you defile or cheat, or whatever you ominous people like to do."

"I'll show you what we ominous people enjoy doing." He grabbed her and pulled her against him, her breasts plush against his chest. He strained to resist, but failed. Grasping her chin, Griffin planted his lips over hers. She tasted like raspberries and smelled of soap, her lips soft and delicious.

Cold, mushy ice cream dripped down his shirt front; he jerked away. "You little devil. You've soiled my fine Holland shirt."

"You deserved it, you cad." She shoved the spoon down his shirt neck and the metal chilled his flesh. "And that is the last kiss you'll ever have from me, even if it wasn't half bad!" She turned and pushed her way through the bushes, back to the pavilion.

"Don't deny you enjoyed it immensely," he replied, angry that he should have reined in his emotions—weak emotions he hadn't been aware of before this. "And now I'm certain I'll *have* you...one day, when I have the time to put a leash on you, and a muzzle." Teeth gritted, he pulled out the spoon and tossed it in the grass. Fingers sticky, he headed for the front entrance just as a whistle blew.

At this signal, servants in strategic places lit numerous oil lamps—emblazoning the entire garden. Lovers and strumpets hid their faces. Everyone else gasped in wonder.

Griffin pulled his felt bicorn hat low, swept his cape around him, and hurried for the Thames to the Vauxhall Stairs.

****

In his stuffy office, crammed with ledgers and papers, documents and glass-fronted bookcases, Griffin's man of business said, "You seem distracted, sir. Is anything troubling you? Other than our prohibited manipulations?"

Griffin leaned back in the leather, wing-back chair; a chair designed this way to deter drafts in cavernous manor houses. "Nothing that wouldn't improve with a good spanking." He sighed; why couldn't he get that spiteful-tongued heiress out of his mind? "At any rate, back to business. Are you certain the items in question are ready to be, ah, covertly shipped?"

"That is what this last, cleverly-coded letter said." The man rustled paper as he perused the missive. "The authorities aren't yet certain if it's entirely wrong to smuggle a country's own ruins and relics to another country. But if we prevail, the money will be profitable, without paying the import taxes."

"Good, good. I also have some contraband stowed at Jamaica Inn that needs a buyer—several silver antoninianus's from the second century, before the coins were debased to bronze." Griffin straightened and stared around the well-appointed, if disorganized office. "I don't need the profits, but the high adventure of it is what matters." He was bored with life, sometimes even bored with sheep, and this provided an added spark, as did the other, that creature he wished would vanish and stop tantalizing his dreams. "Well, have my man in the field set it up, so it all goes smoothly in Italy, and we evade the revenue men. I must be off to Cornwall, to make ready at that end." He stood and smoothed down his elegantly-tailored frock coat. "I could go to White's here in town, but that men's only club is a haven for drinkers and gamblers. I think I'll visit Mayfair first, to see a woman about a girl."

"A love interest, sir?" His man looked hopeful. "Are you weary of serving wenches?"

"Hardly. There's nothing like a good wench, whether from a tavern or a farm." Griffin chuckled without mirth. He hadn't bedded as many women as he led people to believe. "This is a game, this current not-quite an *affair de amour*, I must admit. And I so hate to lose at games."

Outside, he hailed a hackney. What a *faux pas*; he should never have kissed that evil child. Three days had passed since Vauxhall. Earl Pencavel had warned him his errant daughter was most likely in Mayfair with her aunt, so he'd had the place watched by trusted minions, thus his ability to track her to Vauxhall.

Riding in the hackney, Griffin ruminated on his life. A staid upbringing, the correct schools, the right tutors, select friends, all so very upper echelon. And as predictable as could be. After inheriting Merther Manor and other estates, he'd be quite the catch as Viscount of Merther, if he allowed anyone near him. But since saddled with this chit his father had drunkenly (his strait-laced father's only vice) agreed to when she was just a babe—and Griffin off in school learning to be the proper Englishman—he'd been safely betrothed and not subject to the slobberings of fat mothers wishing to foist their eligible, giggly daughters off on him.

He'd traveled to Langoron House with every intention of refusing the betrothal and paying off the father to ease his humiliation, but... He hadn't counted on the brat to be so lovely, and contrary, fueling his desire. He clenched his fingers in his soft suede gloves.

She had mentioned excavations, and his sinister inclinations, but surely she knew nothing about his activities.

Of course, he could never marry an astute girl and keep up his smuggling enterprise, but he might have a fling with her. She obviously cared little about her reputation.

In Grosvenor Square, he alighted at the Penpol address.

The ubiquitous somber butler showed him to a parlor, decorated in the passé rococo style of shells, arabesques and elaborate curves in the decor. Even a fanciful Watteau painting of frolicking ladies hung on the wall.

A curvaceous older woman sauntered in, quizzing glass raised. "Lord Lambrick, I presume?" Her lips quirked. Her cheeks were streaked with scarlet rouge. A black velvet beauty patch, or *mouche*, was pasted on her right cheek. "You should have left your card, as is appropriate, then waited to see if I was 'at home'. As you can ascertain, I am. We were not expecting you, yet here you are."

"I'm quite aware of that; do excuse my intrusion, Lady Penpol." He bowed at the proper level for a woman of her station. Her banter amused him, but he wouldn't let on. "I was in town, and wished to see my betrothed, Lady Pencavel."

"But does she wish to see you, is the question. My niece told me she's refused you." The woman's brows arched, her forehead pushing at her mountain of apple-pomaded brown hair, her little lace cap quivering. "You do look like a rogue, if a very fine-looking one, but I digress."

"I see all of your family—the females at least—have quick tongues." He softened his retort with his most charming smile. He could be charismatic when he tried. "And are substantially easy on the eye as well."

"Oh, my. Such flummery, sir." She fluttered her eyelashes. "You are a naughty one. Still, I'm not a green girl to fall for the dulcet tones of a practiced *bon vivant*."

"I concede to your superiority, Lady Penpol. May I have a moment with Lady Pencavel?" He tried a look of contrition, something he was never good at. Inside he cringed at the lengths he had to go to preserve protocol. "I promise I will be brief."

"Very well. My niece swears she's done with you, but it's true she did *not* behave in the acceptable manner. I'll see if she will receive you." The woman ran her pointed gaze over him. "Hmmm, you don't appear to be a man who is so easily discarded." Lady Penpol swished from the parlor.

Minutes later, Miss Pencavel entered in a plain dress of pastel yellow, and she still looked comely, damn her! Her honey-blonde hair waved attractively around her perfect oval face.

"I hope you are here to apologize for your ungentlemanly behavior at Vauxhall." She said it in a way that intimated she hadn't been overly insulted. Her eyes gleamed. "And you intend to 'officially' release me from our obligation."

"I'm pondering one but not the other," he said enigmatically. He could smell her light lemon scent, and his pulse increased. "I took you for a woman of experience."

"Then I should be utterly inappropriate for you. Nevertheless, I am *not* a light-skirt." Her fingers touched the gauzy kerchief around her throat; the cloth that hid her delectable décolletage. "I have nothing to say to you, although we seem to be having a discourse at the moment. Why are you here, exactly?"

"I came to inform you that I've regretted this betrothal since my father told me about it. And after meeting you, I regret it even further." He gave her a cocky smile, but drank her in like a man dying of thirst and hated himself for it.

"I'm so glad I've not lived up to your expectations. It's true that no man will ever claim my heart, but I especially don't want you to have access to it." She lowered her long sweeping eyelashes.

A maid rattled in a tea tray and set it down. Miss Pencavel dismissed her.

"Then we are in agreement." He was thrilled that she continued to spar with him. He had to admit this was why he'd come today, to watch her pretty mouth—the lips he'd enjoyed— deride him. "If you wish to marry some fatuous blockhead who will be flattered by your doubtful charms, then I *might* consent to release you, since I'm not the marrying kind, at least not to someone like you."

"I will never marry and allow any man to preside over me. The ridiculous English laws that give the husband all rights, and the wife none, will never tie me down. Tea?" She poured the liquid into Worcester Porcelain soft-paste, with added soap rock, cups. The pretty red flowered motif looked strangely natural in her delicate fingers.

"You should be tied down, double-knotted if the truth be known." Griffin accepted the overglazed polychrome enameled cup and sipped the rich beverage. "A fine black tea blend from Twinings, I'm guessing. My compliments to your fashion-stunted aunt."

"I will inform her. And I would say, I hope you choke on it, but that would be carrying rudeness to its limits." She sipped from her own cup.

"You're too kind, my, should I say, most unladylike lady?" He watched her sweet lips on the rim of the cup. He wanted to grab her and kiss her, but restrained himself. "So why did you mention excavations on the day we met?"

"Why do you care? I'd like to unearth antiquities, if it's any of your concern." She set down her cup. "I intend to travel to Italy then on to Greece and Egypt, as soon as I am of age."

He gritted his teeth. She would have interests in the very items he was smuggling. What a bothersome creature. He wanted to throw her on the Louis XV-style velvet settee and ravage her, though decided against it. "I'd advise you to stay safe in England. There is a war going in the event you haven't been enlightened of this fact."

"I read the newssheets, and that only makes it more exciting." She smiled provocatively. "I'm well aware of that Corsican general and his successes over the Austrians in the name of France."

Griffin's heart turned to stone. "Do not mention the blasted French." His brother's face swam before his eyes, but he pulled himself together. "And I insist you stay far away from them."

"See, you already behave like an overprotective, bullying husband. How tiresome, sir." Miss Pencavel titled up her chin, her gaze challenging.

"Ah, you have me there, my dear." He bowed, to hide his grimace. Why did he care whether she was eaten by crocodiles in Egypt? He should leave, instead of being distracted by her slim neck and slimmer white arms. How would her skin feel to his touch? He took a quick sip of tea. "In that case, happy sailing across the channel, and may a thousand fleas nibble on your scorched carcass."

She laughed, and it tingled along his spine. "That is more like it. Now be off with you. I'm sure you have some mistress hidden away here in town that awaits your foul ministrations. I must ready myself for a stimulating evening at Almack's, where many men will worship at my pretty feet. Then we'll see how doubtful my charms are, sir." She tossed her head and half-winked as she floated from the parlor.

Griffin wanted to throw the teapot at her. He rubbed the back of his neck where tension usually coiled. She dug under his skin like the rash of a plague. Well, he'd see about her flirting with a bevy of callow lads at Almack's. He thrust on his hat and tramped from the townhome. He had a whore, an actress, here in town, but right now, she wasn't as alluring as the oh so annoying, Miss Pencavel.

Chapter Five

Why had she baited the scoundrel? Melwyn had no intention of attracting any men here at Almack's. She only wanted to see where the rich and famous played before she took on the arduous, yet satisfying, life of an archeologist.

She glanced around the assembly room with its high, arched windows, simple drapes and plain carpet. Secretly, she searched for dark eyes watching, but Lambrick was not here.

"I'm relieved you agreed to accompany me, Mellie. This is one of the premier marriage marts of society in London for the upper crust, though not everyone is admitted." Aunt Hedra primped at her large white ostrich feather that looked like a flag on a mountain peak. "The Duchess of Dumfort is my sponsor, and thus, yours as well."

"I've told you, to no avail obviously, I have no interest in marriage. Besides, even after my discourse with Lord Lambrick, he still hasn't agreed to release me from the betrothal. I acted rashly and so want things above-board for Papa's sake." Why did that rascal of a viscount linger in her thoughts? His fervent kiss had fluttered her heart.

Melwyn shook that aside as she walked with her aunt past milling people who laughed, talked, and sipped wine and tea. The scents of perfumed ladies, men in fragrances of bergamot and sandalwood, and many with body odors less than flattering, swirled around her. "But on another troubling subject, you really should reconsider your hair, Auntie; it is so 1770's, not 1790's. How many *toques* of cork do you have hidden under there?"

"My hairstyle is an elegant pouf, *à la frivolité*." Her aunt twirled the tiny birdcage that dangled from her tresses. "Now, coxcombs play Hazard in the gaming room over there; and there's a supper room, which serves a light repast, and a ballroom for dancing reels and minuets." She pointed with her silk fan. "This is one of the few clubs to admit ladies, and the ladies preside over it in many ways."

"If women only dally here to scout for husbands, I'm afraid this isn't the place for me. I'd prefer a society to discuss the sciences and new discoveries, such as the planet Uranus." Melwyn primped at her hairstyle for emphasis—on the hair, not Uranus—her loose curls attractive under a white turban. Her robe *á la Turque* overdress was of light blue muslin, trimmed in aqua rosettes. Her white petticoat trimmed in pink rosettes peeked out from the folds. "You never did introduce me to your Royal Society friend."

"My dear, when you crawled out of the bushes with scratches on your arms, your hair in disarray, and your lips bruised as if kissing someone, I was loath to introduce you to anyone." Her aunt sniffed and fanned herself.

"There you are, my exquisites." The Duchess of Dumfort wobbled over to them with two towering feathers in her silver tresses that almost tipped over her squat frame. "I have several young men I'd like to present to your beautiful niece. I'm so glad she *is* beautiful. Ugly girls, even if they are heiresses, are difficult to promote."

"Are any of them intelligent? I might chance a conversation, if it is scintillating." Melwyn sighed, allowing the duchess to take her arm to humor her aunt. As they passed through the crowd, a tall man in dark clothing caught the corner of Melwyn's eye. Her heart jumped. She slowed and turned, but no one was there, only a door ajar that led out to a terrace.

"This is Mr. Showreynolds, his father is a baron." The duchess stood Melwyn in front of a stocky man with sandy hair; he appeared to be in his late twenties. "Mr. Showreynolds, this is Lady Melwyn Pencavel."

"I'm honored to meet you, my lady." The pudding-faced young man, who had no remarkable features, took her hand and kissed it.

His sloppy lips felt nothing like Lord Lambrick's sweltering kiss at Vauxhall. Melwyn trembled as she remembered it—again! "How passably nice to make your acquaintance. What do you know of Uranus?"

He blinked his dull eyes, once, twice. "I....uh...I'm not certain what you mean. Is that a jest?"

"Never mind. Pray, please walk with me out to the terrace." She grasped his arm and towed him in that direction. If Lambrick was here, she'd incite his jealousy; however, why she'd want to remained unclear to her.

The cool air, with the less than salubrious fragrances of London, greeted her when she stepped out. Night had fallen and crickets chirped in the bushes below.

"This is highly irregular, we've only just met, Miss Pencavel." The bland Mr. Showreynolds stared at her askance as he stumbled beside her.

"What do you think of the new dog tax to finance the war?" she asked. Her abrupt questions to prospective beaux always befuddled them. This young man was no exception. "Dogs are deemed a luxury, and eat food better needed for the poor."

"I'm certain the g-government knows what's best," Showreynolds stammered.

"I think it's sad, like taxing a friend." She was bored with the baron's son already. "Please, fetch me a cool drink, a lemonade would be perfect. I feel desperately faint." She let him go and staggered to the balustrade, her hand on her forehead in a dramatic gesture.

"By jingo. Do you need a burnt feather waved under your nose, my lady?" He slid backwards as if in fear.

"Hurry, I tell you, bring me the drink. I'm slipping down to the ground." She waved him off. When he returned she'd act friendlier, if needs be.

"As you wish." The nervous never-a-beau-for-her rushed inside.

She dug her fingers into the rough stone of the balustrade. Auntie may be swooning now after this improper display. Since she was a child Melwyn had had trouble with impulse control. She was certain it was because of her mother's erratic behavior, then her abrupt leaving with the lascivious servant for parts unknown. Why hadn't she ever written, not one solitary word, to her only child? Melwyn sighed. She used her acid tongue to ward off her feelings of insecurity at not being good enough for her own mother.

She closed her eyes and shed off the self-pity, which never would get her anywhere, least of all out of England to exotic lands.

A hand touched her shoulder and she spun around. "Back so soon, Mr....?" She gasped, staring up into the ebony pools of Lord Lambrick's eyes. She shuddered with excitement.

"Disappointed, my little scamp?" He smiled slowly. "Were you planning to seduce that chucklehead who was with you a moment ago?"

A spark tingled low in her stomach. "Do you stalk me everywhere, sir? There should be a law against it." She swallowed hard as he leaned over her. "I'm calling a Bow Street Runner to haul you off to the Newgate gaol."

"If you wish to seduce someone, make your first time—if it is indeed your *first* time—with a man who knows what he's doing." He gripped her shoulders.

"You're a dissolute churl, and I should slap your face." She raised her hand, really anxious to stroke his manly jaw. His warm hands sent delightful quivers through her.

"Slap away, my dear, I might enjoy it. And I intend to partake of you." He jerked her against him; she felt his heart hammering into her breasts. He actually *did* desire her. Her knees grew weak, until she regained her senses.

"I'll go to my death a virgin. Unless I find an intriguing Egyptian, a long-dead pharaoh come back to life, or a swarthy camel guide, anyone but *you*, sir." She heaved against him, her breath sharp. He smelled heavenly, like the wind and earth. That first kiss in the garden had been delicious, but she'd never admit it.

She waited, and waited. Finally, he dipped his head and kissed her so passionately, she thought she'd melt. Instead of resisting, she relished in his soft yet demanding lips against hers, the taste of his breath. Her body quaked, filled with the rushing of blood through her veins.

"Uh, here is your l-lemonade, my lady," a tentative voice uttered.

They kissed a few seconds more, then broke apart, gasping for air.

Melwyn practically collapsed against the balustrade. Her body felt thoroughly plundered, or at least her mouth did. "Oh, good evening, Mr. Show...reynolds, was it? Let me introduce you to my...a family friend." She refused to give Lambrick the respect of calling him her betrothed.

"You have a-a very close family, I must say," the young man sputtered. The glass of yellow liquid in his hand shook.

Lambrick plucked the glass from him. "If I ever catch you anywhere near Lady Pencavel again, I'll thrash you beyond recognition. Is that understood?"

"Most certainly, sir. Yet I-I'm thoroughly insulted by both of you. I give you good eve." He whipped about and scrambled through the doors.

"I suppose you will follow me about and threaten to thrash every man who pays me the least attention?" She snatched the glass and drank the cool drink, tart and refreshing on her parched throat. She needed to drench the taste of him from her mouth.

"As arresting as that sounds, I won't have time for such endeavors. I must return to Cornwall." His eyes glinted in the moonlight, his flushed face even more handsome. He gave her a smug smile. "I have a better proposition. Will you spend the night with me, tonight?"

"You are a rascal of the worst sort, and a terrible listener. I told you not five minutes ago that I'd never give you the benefit of my maidenly parts." Inside, she wished he'd pick her up, throw her over his shoulder and carry her off through the garden to force himself on her in a shadowy alley. Then it would be his fault she was disgraced. Of course, then he'd have to offer to marry her, and they'd be right back to the original conundrum.

"What is going on out here?" came the imperious voice of Aunt Hedra. "Have you found a young man to your liking? Even so, you should not loiter out here too long, people will talk. Some are gossiping already." She raised her quizzing glass. "Oh, it's you Lord Lambrick. Why are you here bothering my niece?"

"I don't think she minded, Lady Penpol." Lambrick bowed to her aunt then turned back to

Melwyn. "Mark my words, Lady Pencavel, I *will* have you someday. Maybe not tonight, or even tomorrow, but soon, very soon," he whispered. "And I abhor the dog tax." He touched her cheek, doffed his hat to Aunt Hedra, then bounded down the terrace steps and vanished into the moonlit garden.

Melwyn groaned, her heart pattering like a drum, or a bugle during a call to arms. That horrid, but extremely sexy, man was growing on her like lichen. How soon could she escape the country to save herself?

Chapter Six

Griffin's valet, a massive block of a young man who'd been with him for six years— raised up from the position of footman after he'd proven his loyal nature— stirred the dish of shaving paste.

"Is my new razor sharp?" Griffin ran his hand along his bristly chin. The well-appointed inn where they stayed in Moorgate had solid mahogany furniture and a four-post bed piled high with feather mattresses, which he would unfortunately share with no one. The Italian, giltwood mirror he stared into was of good manufacture as well. He frowned. He didn't appear any different, yet life had taken on a mesmerizing meaning he couldn't define. "The razor touted to be made on 'philosophical principles'? Of all the nonsense."

"Of course, sir. And I've studied Benjamin Kingsbury's *Treatise on the Use and Management of a Razor,* as you instructed." Kenver's square, but handsome face under light brown hair, broke into a smile. "That Huguenot in Pall Mall, Mr. Savigny, promised the sharpest crucible steel, that he did. And the Fleet Street perfumer swore his paste was the best."

"All the London shopkeepers claim their wares are the finest." Griffin tried to push his mind to other things, and away from one troubling gamine. Why was he still here, and not leaving for Cornwall? "A man in these times is viewed as eccentric or worse if unshaven.

A beard is for a hermit, or only worn on religious terms."

"Wise, as always, sir. And I appreciate you allowing me to learn along with you, and improving my speech." Kenver began to lather the pasty soap over Griffin's face.

"Well, it's a trial when you—meaning aristocrats such as I, and nobles—can't understand the King's English after being garbled through regional influences."

The smell of olive oil and fragrant spices was pleasing, playing down the scent of animal fat.

"Right you are." Kenver chuckled. "How was your night at Almack's, sir? You've never said."

Griffin fought a sigh. Why had he kissed Miss Pencavel, *again,* two nights ago? He'd seen her with that milksop of a baron's son, and had to possess her out on the terrace. He'd really wanted to cart her off and have his way with her in the bushes, but damned protocol prevented it. And he'd never bed an unwilling woman.

"An eventful evening, if distracting me from what I should do, which is to return home." He clenched his fist around the cushiony edges of his velvet dressing gown. "I have no time for such frivolities."

"Are we returning to Merther Manor, sir?" The valet smeared more paste on his master's neck.

The warmth against Griffin's skin soothed his fractured emotions.

"Not yet. Go down to the kitchen and choose my steak for later this evening, but no honey sauce. I suppose I must suffer the sooty vegetables boiled in a pan." Griffin had no appetite, but his mind raced in circles. "If there's nothing decent here, we will go to a tavern for a table *d'hôte.*"

"Why do you quality use those snooty French sayings, when we hate the French, sir?" Kenver began to run the sharp blade along Griffin's beard, scraping away the hair.

Griffin bristled, as he usually did at the mention of anything to do with the French. He heard in his memory the cheerful laughter of his brother when they were children. But he had to remain calm while being shaved. "Good point, my man." He snatched the razor—so much for calmness. "Most men shave themselves now. I'm too restless to stand still for this." He quickly skimmed the blade along his neck, chin and cheeks, leaving a few dots of blood. "Sorry to be so abrupt, even if I don't need to explain myself to a servant."

"You're in a highly disgruntled mood, sir." Kenver handed him a towel.

Griffin rubbed the cloth over his face. "So I am. I think I'll take a quick ride in the park to clear my head."

"Before that, sir." Kenver set down the dish, and the returned razor, on the wash stand. "A man approached me down in the common room. He says he wants to meet with you tomorrow, outside London on the Great North Road in Islington. There's a—"

"And why does this person wish to meet with me?" Griffin pulled on his buff leather riding breeches over cream clocked stockings, fine silk shirt and leather riding jacket with frogged buttons.

"I'm getting to that, sir." His valet glanced around as if they weren't alone in the chamber. "He says he has something important you might wish to buy."

"Everyone seems to know my extra-curricular activities." Griffin hid his leeriness over meeting with another stranger. He waved his valet's assistance away and jerked on his dark leather jockey boots.

"He assured me these items will bring much profits." Kenver frowned thoughtfully. "But he seemed a sleazy type to me, so I'd be cautious."

"I do need to build new cottages for my tenants, to make their lives more comfortable. Very well, tell him I'll meet him in a public place. Get the particulars." Griffin donned his cape and something else he kept concealed from Kenver.

Outside in the corridor, Griffin dropped a few coins into a box mounted there with the words, To Insure Prompt Service, abbreviated as TIPS.

He'd gallop on a hired stallion, and maybe find something or *someone* to garner his fevered attention, and blur his desire for Miss Pencavel.

****

"You're a bit drab lately, m'lady." Clowenna brushed rosemary over Melwyn's over tunic to sweeten the garment after using lye and kerosene to treat a stain. "An' far too quiet these past two days, which ain't like 'ee at all. Even as me ears is enjoyin' it."

"And you never silence your jaw, do you, Clowie?" Melwyn reclined on her bed in Aunt Hedra's guest chamber and turned the page of *Le Antichità di Ercolano,* the folio collection of the archaeological discoveries of Pompeii and Herculaneum. The book was beautifully illustrated, but didn't hold her interest as it usually did. This latest volume had been published in 1792, however, all she could think about were mahogany eyes and a deep, cultured, if oh so mocking, voice. "I think I might leave you on the mean streets of London to fend for yourself. You could be a mud lark, perhaps."

"I'm too old to scavenge in the river mud for booty." Her abigail bent over the book, her round face thoughtful. "Teach me some o' that Eyetalion, if I'm to go wi' 'ee to Italy."

"I detest it when you're right." Melwyn slammed the book shut with a slap. "Nevertheless, I'm in no mood to teach one who had no education in the first place, as servants aren't bothered to be educated, especially women, as unfortunate as that may be." She softened her rhetoric. "I'll teach you later if you behave."

"'Tis true. People is afeared we low-borne might get airs above ourselves, isn't they?" Clowenna fluffed out a feather on her lady's straw hat. "Instead, lessons be wasted on privileged toffs like 'ee."

"Mine weren't wasted. At least they won't be if I can tweeze that thorn of a scoundrel out of my life." She'd almost said "heart" but the idea stunned her. She couldn't be falling in love with Lord Lambrick. She trembled. Oh the dreadfulness of it! She nearly fell off the soft feather mattress under its intricately carved rococo headboard.

"That be the gist of your melancholy, m'lady?" Clowenna hauled up the chamber pot from under the bed. She opened the closest window. "Are 'ee that sad his lordship follows about an' harasses, or that he said he left for Cornwall, an' cannot harass 'ee no more?"

Melwyn wrapped her flimsy nightgown around her, tucked her feet under her and tapped her cheek in thought. Torrid lips on hers invaded her memory, making her quiver. "You've come to the nucleus of the problem, I must admit."

"Whatever 'nucleus' might mean." Clowenna leaned out the window. "*Garde à l'eau!*" she shouted before dumping the pot's contents. "Oh, la, I might o' hit the muckraker; but at least he's there to tidy up."

"I'm certain I'm only distracted by that cur of a lordship's ruthlessness, nothing more. He only wants a doxy, which I am not." Melwyn stood, fighting the sag of her heart. "Brush off my finest riding habit. I'm to ride a hired horse in Hyde Park, while Auntie and the duchess trundle along in a carriage, following me as killjoy chaperones."

"I'm all agog at your finally goin' out." Clowenna opened the clothes press where garments were neatly folded. "Don't embarrass them too much, m'lady. O' course that be too much to ask."

Along Rotten Row, through the stately oaks of the park, Melwyn sat awkwardly in the side saddle her aunt insisted she had to utilize. The broad bay mare undulated beneath her, clopping evenly, snorting occasionally, the scent of horse sweat sharp.

Red poppies and yellow buttercups sprinkled the stretch of lawn that surrounded the Serpentine pond where geese fluttered about like...geese in the April air. The flowers' light fragrance mixed with the mossy smell of the park.

She squirmed on the saddle, the pummel digging into her draped-over leg. At home at Langoron House she rode astride like a boy, though never when her father watched. The groom didn't mind allowing her this freedom. Still, it rankled her that she was so suppressed as a female she had to think of it as an *allowed* freedom, rather than her due as a person.

In Italy and Greece she'd pass herself off as a widow, since those women were given more leeway in their actions. She laughed softly. Every high-spirited young lady should pretend to have a dead husband.

She kicked the horse's flank, and the mare cantered away from the following carriage, where Aunt Hedra and the Duchess of Dumfort prattled on about a subject that was far less than stimulating, Melwyn was assured.

She reveled in the motion of the horse, her own swaying hips and shoulders, the breeze caressing her face. The sun warmed her back. Birds squawked in the branches above her, but why did she search the area, the other riders, for the brooding form of Lord Lambrick? He should be well on his way back to Cornwall by now.

"Do wait up, Mellie, darling!" Aunt Hedra stuck her head out the window, her mound of hair barely moving in the wind, her hat flapping atop like a trapped bird. "I'm meeting my Royal Society friend over near Speakers' Corner. You did want to be introduced, didn't you?"

Melwyn reined in her horse, turned the mare around and joined the ladies. "You promised me at Vauxhall to meet this illustrious person. I wonder if you tease me, and made him up, Auntie dear."

"Is this a ghost?" the duchess asked, her ringed fingers clicking together. "How delightful, I love ghosts. Yet no one has shown me an actual one, so that I might be convinced they are real. Regardless, they must be well-behaved spirits; no chain rattlings and the like."

"No, no, your grace, he is very real; that is, he's not a ghost." Aunt Hedra tapped on the coach ceiling. "Head for Speakers' Corner, please, driver."

Melwyn followed the coach, still scanning the park for anyone who might be watching her, such as a certain rakehell she had no interest in meeting up with.

"I'm trying to mollify my niece, your grace," Aunt Hedra whispered in the coach, though Melwyn heard her plainly. "She has foolish notions of grave digging, or some such rot, in foreign climes, and refuses to marry. My poor milquetoast of a brother wishes her safely married, and settled—as all good fathers would."

"Grave digging? How repulsive. You must nip that in the bud at the onset," the fatuous duchess replied in shocked tones. "Is *that* where we uncover the ghost, in a grave? Then I have no wish to be a part of it."

Melwyn stifled a laugh as they neared the far corner of the park. Here, anyone, quality or no, could stand and expound on any subject they preferred.

"We'll have to make sure the gel never gets a passport," Aunt Hedra said with a slap of her fan. "I don't understand why she is so against accepting her lot in life as a female."

"My husband, the duke, insists that Bath is full of such uncultivated women, and he's forbidden me from joining him there because of it; bad influences and all that entails," the duchess prattled on in her safe ignorance as the coach stopped.

"I'm certain your venerable spouse keeps busy reading religious tracts," Aunt Hedra replied with an arched mouse skin-covered eyebrow. If she hadn't shaved off her own, as was the past fashion, she wouldn't need these bizarre replacements.

The driver jumped from the box, let down the step, and Aunt Hedra alighted.

"Isn't your niece betrothed to that dashing rascal, Lord Lambrick?" the duchess asked as she squeezed her voluminous skirts from the coach with the driver's assistance; her outmoded panniers rattled like the chains she'd rebuked. "Though she did seem interested in that young man I introduced her to at Almack's."

"I doubt that lamentable boy will hold my niece's attentions for half a second." Aunt Hedra motioned to the driver, who now assisted Melwyn down from her mount in the middle of her struggles to dismount by herself. "She requires a decidedly stronger hand."

"I require no hand but my own," Melwyn intoned. "Weren't the Old Tyburn Gallows near here?" She brushed down the skirt of her lavender habit.

"There must be many frightening ghouls lurking about, unfairly hanged over the centuries, anxious for revenge."

The duchess gasped and held a handkerchief to her nose as if the stinking corpses might rise from the earth at that instant. "Upon my word. Young ladies certainly have changed since I was at finishing school. I would have had no knowledge of hangings." She pulled a small, silver vinaigrette box from her sleeve and opened the hinged lid. "I need my smelling salts."

Aunt Hedra dragged Melwyn close, painfully close. "You are incorrigible, my dear. Definitely inherited from your regrettable mother's side of the family. Now, here is my friend, Mr. Fernworthy, the scientist."

A rotund man stood there, his belly protruding from under a tight waistcoat that strained at its buttons. His nankeen breeches seemed to barely contain his wide thighs. He pinched his pince-nez over a bulbous nose. "My dear Hedra, always so good to see you. Terrible thing about Penpol; liked the man, I truly did. But ashes to ashes and dust to dust, as is written." He greeted and bowed to the duchess in turn.

"That was five years ago I lost dear Penpol, Fernworthy. Do keep up." Aunt Hedra sighed, her roughed lips in a twist. "Anyway, I asked you here to speak with my niece and show her the folly of her ways. She wants to go to digs."

At that moment, a tall man in a black cape ascended the block of stone, designating a speech was about to begin.

"Excavations, to be correct, Auntie. I wish to be part of unearthing ancient treasures, and lost cities, Mr. Fernworthy." Melwyn scrutinized the man on the block, at first thinking it was Lord Lambrick playing a trick on her. Her heart twinged. But, alas, he wasn't handsome at all, and distinctly drunk, judging by the way he weaved.

"Eh, are you speaking of archeological excavations?" Fernworthy leered at her. "But you're a woman, in case you haven't noticed. No women are allowed there. Bad form to even think of it."

"Thank goodness." The duchess clasped her chest. "Grave digging is reprehensible, and filthy. Once someone's in the ground, they need to stay there."

"Bodies are needed for medical science!" the drunk on the block announced in a slurred voice. "Even *if* it is against the law."

"Would any women be allowed to even witness an excavation?" Aunt Hedra persisted, then whispered to her male friend, "Make it sound as odious as possible."

"Well, I am a botanist not an archeologist, but I can say, without any qualm, that no woman would be allowed anywhere near such a...*odious* undertaking. Too dusty, and dangerous. And I hear the ones in Pompeii have lewd graffiti on the walls." Fernworthy eyed Melwyn as if she sprouted two noses. "Be a good girl and go home, marry and have a dozen children."

"Botany? An overrated gardener? Many women have excelled in that vocation, sir. Such as the Countess of Strathmore." Melwyn smiled, while inside she cringed. She walked away from the supercilious gnome.

"And women are multi-talented. I've read that in America, the natives strap their babies to their backs, and continue to weave baskets, create beaded necklaces, work in the fields, and skin buffalo."

"All womanly tasks, so your example falls flat." Fernworthy snorted, then confided to Hedra, "No one will marry her, unless they'd first cut out her argumentative tongue. They never should have taught women to read, therefore to think, and dare to speak on subjects they know nothing about, very bad form. The Royal Society, founded in the previous century, is full of philosophers who promote knowledge, but not for addle-brained females."

"I take exception to that, Mr. Fernworthy. Why keep women ignorant, so men may dominate us? It shores up your own insecurities and proves your lack of enlightened moral fiber." Melwyn glared at the pompous botanist. "I shall send you a copy of Mary Wollstonecraft's *A Vindication of the Rights of Woman: with Strictures on Political and Moral Subjects*."

"And she's witty, lovely to look at, and luscious to kiss, I'll be bound," the drunk crooned as he swayed.

Melwyn eyed the soused speaker in annoyance. "Stay out of this, sir! You are clearly foundering in your cups."

The stranger jumped from the block, snatched Melwyn around the waist, and ran to a waiting horse hidden behind a tree. He hoisted her up, climbed on behind her, discarded his ugly mask, and rode off, holding her tightly.

"That inebriated fellow just tore off his own face!" The duchess swooned and Fernworthy caught her, but they rolled to the ground like two water-filled sheep's bladders.

"Very curious, indeed." Aunt Hedra raised her quizzing glass and glared at the departing stallion. "That man looks peculiarly familiar."

Melwyn struggled for breath, in much too much shock to think rationally as she wriggled to be free of muscular arms.

Chapter Seven

She felt so soft and warm against him, though she squiggled so much Griffin could barely concentrate on the galloping stallion between his thighs.

"Hold still, you hellion! I don't wish to harm you." He grimaced. "But if you keep struggling, I may have to."

"Unhand me, sir. What in darnation do you think you're doing?" Miss Pencavel pinched at his fingers through his suede leather gloves. "I am completely flummoxed, and much put out, and these coincidences are becoming pathetic."

Griffin slowed his horse on the other side of the huge expanse of Hyde Park, near the brick edifice of Kensington Palace, a renovated Jacobean mansion now used by lesser royalty. "I'm kidnapping you, you little idiot."

"But why? Why do you follow me like a hound dog chasing a bitch in heat? And I'm certainly *not* in heat." Her narrow shoulders struck back at him in her tailored riding habit jacket.

"Such foul words, my lady." He reined in the beast. The horse snorted and slapped his tail. Why was he following her, instead of on his way home to Merther Manor? He had no explanation for his actions, except she had bewitched him. He couldn't possibly care about this bratty baggage. "No prospective groom would be enchanted."

"You *do* want to marry me, don't you?" She said it as an accusation. "But I still don't want to marry anyone, least of all a rapacious ruffian such as you."

"So you keep telling me. I don't relish a wildcat in my bed either." He tamped down the stirrings inside him at her wriggling in his lap. He'd never minded a lusty bedmate, but this young lady was treacherous. "But I think you'll be safer back home in Cornwall. Promise me you'll return to your father as soon as possible."

"I will return when I'm ready and not before." She jerked at his fingers again. "You have no authority over me, and never will."

"If you'd let me finish." The scent of her hair intoxicated him, much more than any brandy. He resisted dipping his nose into her silken locks. "Return home, and we'll discuss this very inconvenient betrothal, with your father present."

"You must assure me that you will refuse me in writing, to soothe my father's sensibilities." Her words sounded hopeful—and he was strangely disappointed. "I can keep my dowry and sail to Italy the day I turn one and twenty."

The idea of her in Italy, with all those swarthy Italian Lotharios galled him. "Whether you retain your dowry is up to your father. In Italy you will fall in with shady types and certainly be taken advantage of. You'll be used, abused, and left with nothing, ending up in rags and begging in the streets of Naples." The idea of anyone else kissing her pouty lips infuriated him. "What do you know of archeology? Aren't you some rich girl playing at being a great explorer?"

"I am quite serious about this endeavor. I've even bought chipping hammers." She turned about as best she could to glare into his face. "I've studied in depth the work of Johann Joachim Winckelmann. He was the founder of scientific archaeology. He first applied empirical categories of style on a systematic basis to the classical history of art and architecture." She tossed her fair head. "If I were a man you would encourage me in my dreams, not discourage me."

"You are a literate creature, and I admit I'm slightly impressed. Nevertheless, I'm only concerned for you." He couldn't stop himself from touching her bottom lip, though should have removed his glove first. "And if you *were* a man I wouldn't want to do this." He framed her face and kissed her, hard, until she gasped for breath and mewled into his mouth. His yearning rose to fever-pitch.

She finally jerked her lips from his. "You overstep yourself, sir. And my neck is twisted in this position. Undoubtedly, you are a perfidious scalawag for 'kidnapping' me for no apparent reason, except you must be mad."

"Mad, perhaps; a scalawag, I've been accused of such before." He chuckled, but wished he could go on kissing her, and much more. He resisted running his fingers through her honey-blonde hair, the sun glinting off the strands. By God, he was besotted, and barmy, and regretted it. He must ride swiftly to Merther Cove to receive his smuggled goods, and let the wind whip this sorceress from his brain. He wanted to shout that he'd release her, to cleanse her from his blood, but refused to give her that satisfaction. He needed time to think. To rally his forces, to keep the upper hand, to stop ranting these trite platitudes to himself.

He gripped her around the waist and lowered her to the ground, reluctant to let her go. "Return home to Cornwall. I will meet you at Langoron House in a fortnight. If you aren't there, I warn you, the betrothal will stand." He kicked the horse's flanks and rode off, past the palace, the palace gardens, through the cool scent of woodland, and away from her enraged blue eyes, like pools of frozen ponds.

****

On Great Russell Street in London's Bloomsbury district, Melwyn climbed the several steps of the British Museum, housed in the slowly deteriorating Montague House. She admired the grand seventeenth-century mansion's façade of seventeen bays, with a slightly projecting three bay centre and three bay ends. The two-storied building had a prominent mansard roof with a dome over the centre.

"I dearly hope that impetuous lout of a viscount has returned to Cornwall, which I refuse to do yet, on principle." Lambrick's threat to her only served to stiffen her resolve to ignore him...for a time. His last kiss had curled her toes, and confused her mightily. "He can't possibly force me to marry him."

Aunt Hedra followed, adjusting her bonnet—a white and purple striped sarcenet hat, with an embroidered purple border. The item, trimmed round the crown with a rose-colored gauze handkerchief, clung to the top of her hair like a misplaced scarf. "You must stop this stubborn insistence on enriching your mind. Someday you will wish to marry, and you don't want to appear smarter than your husband. Men don't appreciate that. And wasn't Lord Lambrick quite the *bon vivant*, snatching you in the park?"

"He's an unabashed *roué*, who keeps taunting me over this betrothal. And I believe you've misinterpreted the meaning of *bon vivant,* Auntie." Melwyn stared around at shadows as she primped at her demi-gipsy hat, trimmed with green ribands that formed a large bow in the front. "I trust your friend today will be much more deserving of my attention than the pathetic Mr. Fernworthy."

"I will humor your aspirations, or at least pretend to." Aunt Hedra puffed out her cheeks. "Mrs. Anna Bookbinder is a well-known writer here in town, and she expounds on the edification and education of women."

"And she's a member of the Bluestockings, that famous literary circle. I have read a few of her treatises on women's rights: *Measure my Brain as it's the same size as a Man's, and just as Rational, No matter what You've Heard*, was especially enjoyable." Melwyn entered the cool interior of the museum, anxious to visit Sir William Hamilton's collection of Greek and Roman artifacts.

A tall reed-thin woman approached them. "Hedra, good afternoon. This must be your niece. Why, isn't she precious." Her long face with aquiline nose broke into a skeptical smile. "A fledgling archeologist did I hear, young lady?"

"I am indeed honored to meet you, Mrs. Bookbinder. I'm Melwyn Pencavel." Melwyn took in the woman's severe attire, a closed robe grey gown with a starched white kerchief tucked in the bodice. She resembled a nun without the wimple, and was the cliché of a bluestocking.

Melwyn compared it to her own dress, a round gown of striped muslin, the train trimmed with a broad green satin riband; the short full sleeves trimmed with lace. Just because a woman had brains didn't mean she had to look frumpy.

"I'm sure you are, as I am a clever expert in numerous fields, and though a spinster, I rail against marriage as a slavery for women. They can be beaten by their husbands if they misbehave, and *he* determines what constitutes misbehavior." Mrs. Bookbinder nodded her hatchet face. "You must read my newest publication: *A Few Women are only Stupid because their Men have beat them Silly.*"

"That sounds riveting. And is why I'll never marry. Do you delve into the sciences at all?" Melwyn surveyed the famous Warwick Vase, a marble receptacle with intricate Bacchic—wine-related— ornamentation, found at Hadrian's villa in Tivoli.

"Hadrian, was it?" Aunt Hedra raised her quizzing glass. "Wasn't he the man who built the wall to our north to keep out the barbarian Scots? For what good it did."

"I'm so proud of you, Auntie, you *do* listen to my talks on history." Melwyn smiled, genuinely pleased.

"Sciences, you ask? I haven't delved into them personally. But many women have excelled at math. Sadly they're mostly Italians and French, races far inferior to we English." Mrs. Bookbinder stared down her slope of a nose at the Portland Vase. This urn was blue and white cameo and depicted seven figures, one believed to be Paris. "I could use this piece for flowers."

"You're not very open-minded, when it comes to races or vases," Melwyn whispered to herself, so as not to be rude to her aunt's friend—and respect her elders. Another disappointing encounter. "What a beautiful *objet d'art*. I wish I could unearth something as momentous." Melwyn sighed and studied the other artifacts: coins, medallions, jewelry, and bronze sculptures. "Much of this was discovered in Pompeii. I *must* go there. Sir William Hamilton, our illustrious ambassador in Naples, however, believed that vases and sculpture should be left unrestored." She tapped her chin in contemplation. "I'd like to write my own treatise on why women should be included in this new field of archeology and welcomed at the Royal Society."

"I will admit that you're right, Hedra." Mrs. Bookbinder nudged her aunt with a sharp elbow. "She does go on and in my opinion tends to be a braggart. I see no literary merit in the child as she's never been anywhere or accomplished anything."

"Yet you admitted to preaching about the disadvantages of marriage, and *you* have never ventured between the matrimonial sheets," Aunt Hedra reminded her. "Don't be so dismissive of her attributes. I'm afraid the gel is determined, and that's what worries me."

Mrs. Bookbinder snorted. "Don't work yourself into a tizzy. She's too comely, so no one will ever take her seriously. Read my article in last week's *Bluestocking Bulletin*, 'Why a Pretty face often Hides a Flibbertigibbet.'"

Melwyn fought down a stabbing retort. A footstep to the left alerted her. Someone slipped behind a huge statue of Zeus brandishing a lightning bolt. She quivered as visions of Lord Lambrick sprang to mind. Would he grab her here and carry her off like the heathen he was? Why did that excite her?

She tried to peer around Zeus, to catch a glimpse. A figure hurried off, but he was much shorter than the viscount. Could Lambrick change his height at will?

Melwyn slapped a hand on Zeus's marble thigh, deciding it time to return to Cornwall and put an end to these machinations.

****

Griffin entered the tavern, *The Pig and Pickle*, in Highbury in Islington, leaving the reek of cow pens behind as cattle were driven through here on their way to Smithfield.

The dim, low-beamed place smelled of ale and smoke, and rarely scrubbed bodies.

He scanned the faces in the common room, candlelight flickering over sneers and glares. A man wearing a green bandana around his throat, as previously arranged, gestured Griffin over to a corner table.

Griffin stroked the handle of his pistol tucked in his breeches, approached and sat down across from him. "Mr. Shadedeal, I deduce?"

The man lifted the brim of his round hat. He had a pock-marked face with deep lines around his bulging eyes. "Aye. Will you share an ale with me, with you payin' o'course, since you has the higher income?"

"As long as you don't waste my time. I'm on my way home to Cornwall." Griffin waved over a pot-boy and ordered two ales. The drinks arrived and they sipped, watching each other carefully. Griffin wasn't impressed with the house ale as it tasted watered-down. "Now what do you think you might have for me?"

"It's worth its weight in gold, for a man wi' your connections." Mr. Shadedeal stood. "But we'll go in the back where we can talk private-like, an' I'll show you."

"What do you know of my connections?" Griffin rose, wariness prickling on the back of his neck. He followed the man down a short hallway, pondering why a viscount was skulking about seedy taverns, with murky characters, where he could be murdered at any moment. The adrenaline rush, no doubt!

In a fetid back room, Shadedeal pointed to several crates. He pried one open and pulled out a long gun. "I has fifty of the sleekest flint-lock, muzzle-loaded, Charleville muskets."

"Guns? I don't deal in weapons of *any* type. You have been grossly misinformed." Griffin's face heated in anger. "And you show me vile French muskets, named after the armory in Charleville-Mézières, Ardennes, France? These guns are known to be inaccurate in their firing as they are smooth bore barreled."

The man scowled and fingered the walnut stock. "These are standard French infantry muskets, good for firing from mass formations. What matters what you smuggle?"

"It matters. I will never dirty my hands with goods such as these—if I happened to smuggle at all, which I don't admit. And I'll *never* have anything to do with France. Besides, these weapons are slightly smaller than the British made Brown Bess." Griffin turned to leave, his frustration rife.

"Will you report me to the constables?" Shadedeal asked in an accusing voice.

Griffin paused, wishing he could do just that. But any such ministrations would put the spotlight on him and his own fraudulent pursuits. "No. I will leave you to your evil gunrunning."

"I don't believe you. You quality lie an' cheat us poorer folk." The man tenderly placed the musket back in the crate, then lunged at Griffin with a suddenly whipped out knife.

Griffin grabbed the man's arm before the blade nicked his chest. They struggled, wrestling to gain the superior advantage. "Dammit, man, I won't let you kill me. I have a betrothal to overturn, and a damsel to harass. And my tenants count on me to take care of them."

Shadedeal grunted, shoving the knife near Griffin's nose. Griffin saw his life pass before his eyes, and thought, *I still have much more living to accomplish.* He shoved the man away, then punched him in the jaw, sending him crashing to the floor. The knife skittered away against the skirting board.

Griffin snatched out his pistol. Swiping his arm across his now sweaty brow, he said, "I'd shoot you, you worthless brigand, but I don't wish to waste a bullet. And I'm a gentleman, and would never shoot an unarmed man. Stay in that corner and don't follow me." Griffin backed out of the room, pistol pointed. He stalked from the tavern, chiding himself for being a fool to have come here.

Chapter Eight

The Pencavel coach barreled down the London road toward the West Country. Melwyn felt her teeth judder as the wheels hit each bump and rut. She mused again on Miss Bookbinder from the day before. "I see how some women can think they're superior to other women, and nationalities. If I've behaved that way to you, I apologize."

"Did a statue fall on your head in that museum, m'lady?" Clowenna asked in all seriousness from the seat across.

"You're right, why change our relationship now." Melwyn glared out the window as she slumped against the squabs. Rolling green hills, heath and heather and quant villages passed her vision. The air smelled light of foliage and farmland. "At least it's Sunday, and public coaches are forbidden to operate, so we have the road mostly to ourselves."

"You're in a hurry to reach home, an' be rid o' Lord Lambrick for good?" Clowenna picked up the book that her lady had purchased in London.

Melwyn traced a finger down the coach window. "I'm preparing myself for monumental changes. I was rash to leave home. I should have considered my father's feelings. That dumpy duchess is correct in that I will harm my family name if I don't do things properly." She stretched her sore back muscles, regretting that she should have to bow down to any propriety—and she wished she'd ever met the handsome viscount.

"An' what o' goin' off to Italy to dig?" Her abigail watched her with probing eyes as she groaned at another bump. "Won't that harm your father's name?"

"That's why I'll go as a widow...a *faux* widow of course. It would take too much time to marry, and then pray my husband dies the day after." The thought of Lambrick dying filled her with a sudden sadness. Melwyn had feelings for the man she didn't *want* to have. Just remembering his kisses heated her inside like a coal brazier. His deep voice made other parts of her body sizzle as well.

"I think 'ee likes the viscount more than 'ee will admit." Clowenna grinned provokingly. She glanced at the book's illustrations. "What's this epic called again, since 'ee *still* hasn't taught me to read?"

"It's titled *Excavation Exposé, or How to Sneak off to Italy to Explore ancient Strata during Wartime with the Loathsome French.*" Melwyn had been thrilled to purchase this tome at Joseph Johnson's in St. Paul's Churchyard. She prayed she could put it to good use.

"An' what's this pot o' cream for?" Clowenna lifted up the glass jar beside the book.

"Aunt Hedra insisted I take it. It's to keep the skin soft. In countries like Italy and Egypt, the sun is supposed to be merciless." For the first time, Melwyn wondered if she'd ever have the right, or monies, to leave England. Her spirits sagged like wilted petals. Would her father let her have her dowry money? She stuffed away her doubts like swatting at bees. "The cream has spermaceti in it; a product I should know nothing about."

"Ess? I might know somethin', given the nature of me mam." Her abigail said it softly, with a derisive edge to her voice.

"What about your mother?" Melwyn straightened in the seat, her curiosity growing. Clowenna had come to her at the age of almost sixteen, when Melwyn was but ten, and never had mentioned her past before.

"Never mind, m'lady. She's not important." Clowenna's normally ivory skin flushed a shade of pink. She grabbed the wrist strap as the coach lurched. "I'd rather talk o' his lordship."

Melwyn slumped back again, and reluctantly ruminated more on the viscount. "If I do like the man, which I couldn't possibly, it's only a passing fancy." She dug her fingers into the buttery leather seat and hoped to be right. She scanned the road, imagining that a man in a dark cape would ride up at any moment, pretending to be a highwayman, but in actuality would be Lord Lambrick. She shook off that silly fantasy. "Love, or rather I should reiterate just plain 'like' is a weakness that deters one from their true purpose."

"I never said nothin' 'bout *love*." Clowenna snickered in that self-satisfying way of hers.

"A trip of the tongue, you witchy jade." Melwyn crossed her arms in disgust, or was it something else? Why did the mere idea of Lambrick put her out of sorts, trouble her sleep, discombobulate her? She should be eager to end their association.

The coach slowed at a mushroom shaped building, a toll house. The toll-taker ran out and demanded payment from their coach driver. When given, the official opened the gate, which had pikes inserted in the top to prevent people from jumping the gate to avoid paying their fares.

Their coach rambled on, jolting through a rut. "These turnpike trusts are supposed to keep up the roads, but do a poor job," Melwyn grumbled, her mind hardly on road issues, but straying to firm clutches in gardens, on terraces, and on the back of horses.

****

In the shearing shed of Merther Manor, Griffin watched the men, hired shearers who roamed the countryside in search of this type of work, prepare the sheep. He'd enjoyed this as a boy, and now and then peeked in to observe.

He and his brother had lent a hand in the shearing when younger. Those were happy, carefree times, long before the weight of responsibility closed in on them both. His shoulders tightened, aggravating his recent wound. The bruises on his knuckles from hitting Shadedeal had turned yellow, but this new injury was more serious.

Against his surgeon's advice, tomorrow he'd leave for Bodmin to give Miss Pencavel his decision.

The shearers cleaned the wool, removing burrs and other debris as the sheep bleated in annoyance. The air stank of feces and sweating animals. But this was life, not the showy halls of Almack's where dandy fops wasted their days.

One man held the sheep with its skin taut, his hand under the ram's jaw and around its nose. Another sheared its belly with clips of a sharp blade, removing the wool from the breastbone down to it scrotum. The wool came off in wooly bundles, the air soon thick with hair. He sheared around the throat, neck and head, down each shoulder, then the buttock and tail.

"Taking the noose or no, sir?" Jacca came to stand beside him, coughing in the confluence of fuzz. "Not that I can recommend the leg-shackled-to-a-hag state."

"Miss Pencavel is far from a hag, sorry to say." Griffin chuckled dryly. "I'm leaning heavily toward no, but my mind is conflicted, oddly enough."

"Shouldn't o' chased her about in that there London, ess?" His bailiff studied him. "'Ee was courtin' trouble, pardon me spoutin', with that illogical behavior, sir."

The shearer swept aside the mounds of wool, ready for the next sheep. He wiped the gathered lanolin from the previous animal from his blades.

"I don't know what came over me with the girl. She called me mad, and I'm beginning to believe I am." Griffin stepped outside to breathe deeply. He raked his fingers through his hair. "I can't trust myself near her. But hopefully I'll come to my senses and be the clear thinking, callous to women, libertine I've always been." He'd never felt so out of control around a woman before, and he didn't like it for one moment. He clenched his fist.

"How's the shoulder?" Jacca coughed again and spit on the ground. "Had me a mite scared after what happened t'other night. 'Ee probably should o' stayed in bed longer."

Griffin touched his bandaged arm and winced at the pain. "I'm too restive to lounge about like a lazy old hound. Thought I'd lost my life, or at least my reputation. The second such incident in a few days' time. Maybe I'm getting too old for such wildness." Perhaps the nagging hurt in his flesh would keep his mind off the succulent Miss Pencavel.

****

"He made no promise, the blackguard. But he should be here in a day or so to straighten out the situation, then we will decide how to proceed." At Langoron House's dining room table, Melwyn dug her fork into the stinky pickled smelts. Inside, her heart did a strange flutter at the anticipation that she might soon face Lord Lambrick. At night she *still* dreamt of his steamy kisses as her body tingled. Would he coldly dismiss her as his future wife? But wasn't that what she sought all along? She shoved a bite of the densely fishy fish into her mouth, then glanced at her father. "I know how *I* will proceed, but I suppose it should be done appropriately."

"A marriage, how splendidly sweet. However, it isn't proper to refer to your intended as a blackguard." The Widow Whale, a woman as corpulent as her name, simpered. Her neck folds pushed down on the scarf wound around her plump shoulders. She took a bite of the boiled chicken in hog's tongues and stared at Lord Pencavel pointedly, then back to Melwyn. "And never talk with food in your mouth, dear. Especially with fish on your breath."

"We're not at all certain there will be a wedding." Papa sighed lamentingly as he fingered his glass of claret. "My daughter has not been the most cooperative of perspective brides. In fact, she hasn't been the easiest of children to raise, as I have tried to do, as a widower all alone."

"Every woman needs a good man to keep her in line." The Widow popped a piece of duck braised in bacon into her plump mouth. "My late husband always ruled with a strict hand. And *this* abode cries out for a woman's touch. We could plan a double wedding, Pencavel. How quaint that would be. "

"And not very likely with the first wife still alive as far as we know," Bastian whispered as he held a platter near Melwyn's shoulder. "Some hind-saddle of mutton, m'lady?"

"Thank you, Bastian. Papa is still delusional, as you can see." She picked up the serving utensils and dished the gamey-smelling mutton onto her plate. "I don't wish to be the one to dissuade him in his beliefs."

"My Dear Elvira, I have long thought of remarrying, and you would be my premier choice." Her father forced a slice of the duck into his mouth and chewed slowly. "If I'm up to it, woe is me, after all my travails."

"Premier choice? How kind of you to say so, sir." The widow primped at her graying curls with its elaborate toupee. She still wore black trim around her cuffs and edges of her spencer jacket, even though Mr. Whale had been dead for nearly ten years. "Being married is essential for a woman."

"Is it essential? Did you love your husband, Mrs. Whale?" Melwyn asked sardonically. She recalled Mr. Whale as a loud, foul-tempered man, as skinny as his wife was large.

"What has love to do with marriage?" The woman chortled, her beady eyes above fat cheeks squinting. She sucked the marrow from a woodcock bone. "Love is written in silly poems, and frivolous romantic novels, which I'm certain a girl like you must indulge in."

"I'm currently reading the *Le Antichità di Ercolano*; it's fascinating with its copperplate engravings of the ancient Roman artifacts unearthed in Italy," Melwyn took a sip of her claret, the rich red taste comforting, "from the two cities that were entombed for centuries after the eruption of Mount Vesuvius in 79 AD."

The widow blinked several times. "I have no idea what that alludes to. Please pass the fried sausages." She turned to Melwyn's father. "How much money does it take to run your estate? What I mean is, you haven't run through all your funds have you?"

"She means is there any blunt left for her to squander if she could—which she cannot—become Lady Pencavel," Bastian whispered when he served the ragoo of cauliflower to Melwyn.

"You're so perceptive, dear Bastian." Melwyn laughed, easing the tension inside her. "You've been my, well, my bastion, throughout my life. I've long appreciated you."

"You mean I've plucked you from trees, wiped your skinned knees, and once kept you from burning down the house?" The butler never even cracked a smile, yet his eyes twinkled.

Melwyn laughed again, then turned to the widow. "I can refuse this affiancing. I am *allowed* that honor, especially if the man has a less than reputable reputation. And as I told Papa last night, that is what I—"

"You'd be ruined beyond repair, little miss!" The widow waved away the proffered cauliflower, her glower sharp. "You should accept what life gives you and be thankful."

The front door bell rang. Melwyn dropped her fork with a clack. Her heart jumped, and she hated the darned muscle for its traitorous behavior. She resented this man who made her feel like a scatterbrain. "Lambrick *can't* be here now."

"Am I to meet this infamous Lord Lambrick?" The widow looked uncertain, but her gaze turned curious. "I *did* hear he is a man of ill-repute, but not ill-favored."

"Unfortunately, the betrothal was many years ago, before any question of character emerged." Papa sighed and sipped his Madeira, as the claret had run out. "His father was a dear friend, and decent to the highest degree, except for his occasional tippling."

"I will see who it is. Excuse me, sir, Miss and Madam." Bastian left the dining room.

"I'd still like to know what the viscount's less-than-stellar repute is, but no one will tell me." Melwyn hopped to her feet indecorously, scraping back her chair. "I must retire upstairs to spiff myself up. Do excuse me as well." She hoisted her skirts and scurried up the stairs to her chamber.

Clowenna was there sewing the hem of one of Melwyn's gowns. The abigail glanced over in annoyance. "What be 'ee in a fluster about now, m'lady?"

"I think his wicked lordship is here, to either free me with his blessing, or make my life difficult." As she spoke this, she wasn't sure which outcome she wanted. What an enigma! A puzzle of the first magnitude.

"An' now 'ee don't know which to want, ess?" Clowenna stuffed the sewing into her sewing basket. "Should never 'a let him kiss 'ee, what, three times be it now?"

"As if I had a choice. He forced himself on me." Melwyn's body quivered, remembering his smoldering lips, the taste of his breath, his strong fingers kneading her shoulders. "If we weren't betrothed I'd have Papa shoot him."

"Your da couldna tame your mam, so I'd not count on him too much." Her abigail stood and smoothed down her cambric apron. "Now 'ee be hidin' up here under the bed, or goin' out the window? Does 'ee want to shinny down the vines wi' all an' sundry seein' your ankles?"

"Neither, you incessant harpy. I will face the varmint like the stalwart lady I am." Melwyn snatched a brush from her vanity and ran it slowly through her locks.

"You're many things, m'lady, but 'lady' not usually be one o' them." Clowenna snatched the brush and started to style Melwyn's hair. "But we has had our fun, haven't we?"

"And I'm determined to go on doing whatever I wish with no interference, and lug you along with me." Melwyn made up her mind. Lambrick could go to the devil. Other men's kisses could bring her just as much enticement, if she paused long enough between digs to need enticement. "I'll tell my so-called intended I don't intend to bother with him at once."

"I won't hold me breath." Clowenna tried to tie a ribbon in her lady's hair, but was refused. "I think this fellow has dug under your previously hard skin, so to say."

"That shows you how little you know about my fortitude." Melwyn raised her chin, accepted the kerchief to swath around her throat, pinched her cheeks to give them color, then returned downstairs.

In the front hall, her father stood with the Widow Whale and the lean, wind-blown, nefarious form of Lord Lambrick.

He tipped his hat when she approached. "My lady. I am dubiously honored to see you again." His dark eyes drank her in and she couldn't stop a tremor.

"I am somewhat displeased to see you, as well," she replied, her mouth growing dry.

"Oh, they really like each other," the widow cooed as she chewed on a slice of cheese. She nudged Melwyn's father. "You can see it in the sparkle in their eyes. They're trying to hide it, but they are extremely attracted to one another. And he has such a gorgeous patrician profile."

"Mrs. Whale, you are much mistaken." Melwyn frowned, fighting the lift of her heart at Lambrick's hungry assessment of her. "Lord Lambrick and I are tremendously mismatched, and he knows well my feelings."

"I must agree. I have come to the conclusion that a wife, especially one of such inexorable tendencies, would only deter me in my personal plans." Lambrick's voice came out in a monotone. "I will free you with all due respect from the contract."

Melwyn felt the strangest sinking in her stomach. He *was* rejecting her!

"Oh my. I don't know if I should be elated or disheartened. Your father, sir, put great stock in this arrangement." Her father looked at her with sad eyes— though his eyes were most often melancholy. "Now I will have to search for another, more appropriate beau. And with my daughter's, shall we admit, less than malleable deportment—and her insistence on not marrying at all—it may be an impossible feat."

Melwyn smiled. When it came to her, her papa was far from delusional.

"I shall remain a spinster, as detestable as that word is, and continue with my own plans." Melwyn glared at Lambrick, insulted that he dismissed her so easily, but a part of her was relieved. Yet she saw the uncertainty in his eyes, and her confusion added to the complexity of the situation.

"Heaven forefend. If you marry me, Pencavel, I'll take this girl of yours under my thumb and find her a formidable husband to squash that independent will of hers." The widow shook her cheesy finger at Melwyn.

"Leave her be, Madam whoever-you-are." Lambrick glared at the widow. "She is a free spirit, whose wings should not be clipped. Her very truculent, and saucy, nature is what attracts me to her...unfortunately."

Melwyn sucked in her breath. His defense of her weakened her knees. "I appreciate your accolades, I think." Then she turned in reluctance to her father and the widow. "Papa cannot marry you! He is already married!" The words spewed out before she could stop them. She slapped her hand over her mouth and rushed into the parlor.

Lambrick followed her. He hovered close, too close, the fresh air and bergamot scent of him tickling her nose.

"You defend me, yet I'm not good enough to be your wife? How perturbing you are, sir." She said this to keep him at bay; to fend off the effect he had on her. Her heart thumped. He filled out his wide-lapelled frock coat and button-legged pantaloons like a Greek god.

"You are a contrary creature. You warned me you'd never marry me, now you complain because I'm releasing you." He leaned near her face. "However, on this other subject. Your father doesn't realize that his wife ran off with your under-butler?"

"*Second* under-butler. Why does no one ever get this straight?" Melwyn's anger stifled her sadness. She touched a finger to the expensive navy blue wool of his frock coat. "I think Papa retreats into his illusion to help him cope with her desertion."

"A befuddled man; a travesty." Lambrick glanced away; the lines at the corner of his eyes crinkled. "A man should never subordinate himself to a woman." He grasped her hand and held it tightly, massaging her fingers. "It's a terrible weakness."

"I need to point out, sir, that you are standing far too close for a man who just rejected me as his future spouse." She struggled to take an even breath. "Or if you think I will spend the night with you out of wedlock and sacrifice my virginity, you are a brazen fool."

He moved even closer, his gold buttons pressing against her breasts through the flimsy silk of her bodice. "As tempting as that would be, if I wished my face scratched off, I —"

"What finally convinced you to refute the betrothal?" The pressure from his buttons was driving her crazy. She stroked the soft white cravat tied handsomely around his neck. "Not that I don't totally agree with you, and would love to scratch off your face. I only ask out of curiosity."

His hand caressed her upper arm, his fingertips sending delightful sensations throughout her body. His troubled gaze softened and he bent and kissed her heatedly. She gasped at the surging warmth in her chest and lower—much lower. She shivered and was about to hug her arms around his neck.

Then he pulled back. "I cannot tell you, but it happened four days ago. My life is too violent to involve a well-bred, or *should* have been well-bred, young woman. Especially one as intelligent as you." He grimaced in pain. "I have a bullet in my shoulder."

Chapter Nine

Merther Cove, four days earlier

Griffin stood above the shingle beach as the wind whipped about him. His lantern light flickered as the shadows enveloped the landscape. The salty air felt thick, the cold cutting like the knife that gunrunner had wielded through Griffin's caped coat. The sun had set an hour ago and his impatience grew to see the signal that the ship had arrived.

"What could be keeping them?" he grumbled at last.

"Can't predict the waves an' ocean streams. They should be here soon, sir." Jacca thrust his hands in his jacket pockets. Griffin's trusted bailiff pulled out a clay pipe and struggled to light it in the wind. "Hopefully the revenue men won't be sniffing up our arses."

"That's part of the game, now isn't it, Jacca?" Griffin shifted in his jackboots. He held out his cape flap to shield his bailiff, who finally raised a spark with his steel and flint and lit his clay pipe. "The excitement of the sneak, the chase, the undermining of the local authorities."

The surf swooshed against the edges of the cove. A Nightjar trebled as a tamarisk willow whipped its branches.

"Pardon me for mentioning it, sir, but don't 'ee feel a mite guilty not payin' the import taxes?" Jacca puffed on his pipe, the tobacco smell pungent. "Bein' a gentleman an' all."

"Haven't we had this conversation numerous times before?" Griffin raised his spy glass, but could see little out on the dark sea. "George III overtaxed his colonies, and he lost America, didn't he? Then he overtaxed his gentry, which includes me, to pay for the war to bring those rebels under control. Rather, he taxed us *before* he lost the colonies, to pay for his army and navy to secure the colonies, but you understand my meaning. No one likes too many taxes."

"But what's in it for a poor blighter like me?" Smoke swirled about the bailiff's balding head, which was hidden under his round beaver hat whose edges rippled in the gusts.

"You know full well the Cornish profit from smuggling." Griffin wrapped his cloak close. "And you call yourself 'poor?' Are you insinuating that I don't pay you enough?"

"'Tis only a figure o' speech. Damme, 'ee quality is too touchy." Jacca hunched his round shoulders. "An' me wife complains we don't has enough blunt to buy her what she'd like to buy if she was richer. I get an earful o' that every night."

A cormorant screeched off to the right.

"Women, they are a trial to any right-thinking man." Griffin frowned as the face of Lady Pencavel slipped into his mind: her soft pouty lips, golden hair, bright blue eyes, and even softer, svelte body. Why did she disrupt his life? He clenched his fingers around the spy glass. "Why should we tie ourselves up in knots and marry at all?"

"To pass on our name, so to speak." Jacca took another long puff from his pipe. "O' course, 'ee has more reason to want a son, to pass on Merther Manor, an' the hoity toity name o' Lambrick."

"Ah, deuce it all, don't distract me with common sense." Griffin sighed and scuffed his boot along the ground. A pebble skittered down the rocky slope. "Lambrick was *lan-bron-wyk*, my father told me. An 'enclosure of hill wood', of all the bucolic things. The illustrious name is traced to a knight in the thirteenth century."

"Me ancestor were a horse thief in the fourteenth century." Jacca chuckled.

Griffin laughed for the first time in a long while. "Now 'Merther' means a place claiming relics...a saint's relics it's said. And I'm far from a saint." He stared off over the dark sea again, his thoughts in turmoil. "If I can't eradicate the devil from my soul, what right do I have to drag a frail woman into this morass I call my life?"

"'Ee need a hale an' hearty woman, sir. One who wouldn't be afeared o' nothin'. But still can be gentle now an' then, unlike me wife." Jacca snorted in irony. "Not too sure what 'eradicate' means, but 'ee quality like to hide behind them big words."

"And you minions duck behind your vulgar tongue, to keep the rest of us unsure of what you're up to," Griffin muttered.

A light blinked out on the water.

Griffin jerked up the spy glass, thankful to take his mind off of the desirable but atrocious—though admittedly quite hale—Miss Pencavel. "There is a ship, I'm certain of it. God be hoped it is the one we await."

"Why do we care about these ruins from them other countries?" Jacca asked. "Don't we has enough ruins here in England? Me cousin's house is quite the mess, all tumbled down."

"Ancient items bring good money on the black market. I pour that money back into the people here. I don't need it myself, I only enjoy the derring-do." Then why shouldn't he take on a volatile woman for a wife? No, blast it; that would be too precarious. He must let the chit go. Set her free; rid himself of her influence that boiled his blood to a temperature he couldn't handle.

"'Ee could ride the highways an' rob people like that there Robin Hood." Jacca blew a stream of smoke out through his large nostrils.

"Ummm, a little too risky, and hard on the horses, and women and children would be put in danger." Griffin knew he was getting a bit too long in the tooth for such a strenuous venture. Besides, smuggling was a step above a common highwayman.

The light on the water flickered again. Then it blinked three times, paused, and three more times. Griffin pulled up his lantern and repeated the signal.

"That must be her; that were the signal," Jacca said in his infinite wisdom.

"What are we waiting for? Man the skiff," Griffin ordered, his blood thrumming through his veins. This is what life should be about, exhilaration, danger, not bedding some spoiled girl who would nag his ears off and spend his money on fripperies.

Jacca called to the men standing by, and they all tramped down the slope into the cove. A glowworm glimmered greenly in the rushes. The stink of rarely washed bodies wrinkled Griffin's nose. He'd have to donate soap to his tenants and insist on better hygiene.

The shadows lengthened, shortened, the swish of a skiff being pushed out followed. One man grumbled when he got a splinter in his finger. Griffin helped beside the men, his boot toes dampened by the surf.

Oars dipped in water. The ship downloaded crates into the skiff, which almost toppled the boat over. Finally the loot was steadied, the ship's mates paid, and the skiff rowed back into the cove. Griffin raised his lantern to inspect the crates. They were marked with exotic markings confirming they'd come from a foreign port.

"Quickly, pry it open. I want to make certain it contains the correct items."

Rustling came from the hill above them. The sound of footsteps.

A cracking sound. Gunfire!

"Bury the crates in our secret hiding place," Griffin hissed.

Jacca doused his pipe and instructed the men. They lifted a patch of grass that hid a dug out space for just such incidents, and lowered in the crates, replacing the grass, smoothing it down so it resembled the rest of the landscape. Griffin arranged cowslips around the edges.

"Stay where you are!" a gruff voice shouted from above. "We're the king's men!"

"Ignore them, and run and hide," Griffin whispered urgently. His pulse hammered, a smile curving his lips. He reveled in this death-defying occupation. Was this how his brother had felt while facing the French in battle? "I'll hold them off."

"'Ee must save yourself, too, sir." Jacca grasped his arm. "If you're tried an' hanged, I'll lose me position. An' then me old woman won't have no coin at all. I'll never hear the end o' it."

"I'll be fine. Hurry, away with you at once." Griffin pushed the bailiff, who almost lost his footing and toppled into the sea. "I won't see you harmed. My father would roll over in his grave."

"Now *there* were a level-headed bloke, your old man. I respected him, I did." Jacca finally shrugged and vanished into the bushes.

"We know you're down there. Halt in the name of the King!" the gruff voice shouted. "We've muskets and aren't afraid to shoot them."

Griffin stood alone in the bleak darkness, the wind whipping his cape about his legs. He waited until his men's footsteps faded. But the tread from above grew louder. Sweat gathered around his collar. He decided to make a break for it himself, instead of standing here like an idiot.

He turned to run. Another volley of gunfire. A sharp pain cut into his shoulder. Deuce it all, he'd been hit by a bullet. He grabbed his arm, where warm blood pooled, and staggered through the earthy scent of gorse.

Footsteps scrambled down the path above, growing closer. The yells of men chased him as Griffin stumbled around trees and bushes, ducking stray branches, his shoulder on fire. His breath rasped in his throat as he silently cursed his heedlessness.

****

"So you were shot in a hunting accident?" Melwyn wondered if he sought her pity. Lambrick's face looked drawn, and her sympathy did rise, fie! She fought the urge to trail a finger down his chiseled cheek, to hold him close to her breast. "What were you hunting so abysmally?"

"A very rare Italian grouse." He smiled, and her vulnerable heart fluttered.

"What other leisures do you partake of at your estate?" She moved away from him and his appealing cheeks, his infinitely arousing scent. "Murdering innocent creatures couldn't take up all your time."

"That is private, and the reason I don't wish a prying wife in my business." He averted his gaze.

Now he intrigued her. People called him a rogue, but in what way did he deserve that moniker? She'd heard a few whispers as to the truth in London. "You are up to something...illegal, not quite above-board, perhaps?"

Lambrick's dark eyes flashed, his mouth tightening. "Have a care, my dear. Ignorance is bliss. What have you heard, exactly?"

"Nothing specific." She *had* touched a nerve, and his fierce look sent shivers up and down her spine. She ached to know more about him, before she let him disappear from her life. "Everyone calls you a rogue, or infamous, and I was only wondering why."

"Curiosity killed the cat, my lady. In your case, the hellcat." He arched a dark brow, his expression half amused. "Again, more reason to not want a snooping spouse about me, particularly one with your eviscerating tongue."

"Then we are in agreement, our betrothal and any connection between us is null and void." A strange emptiness that he would no longer accost her in parks and pleasure gardens seeped through her. She breathed slowly. "You should be on your way now."

"Do I detect a hint of reluctance on your part?" His voice came out soft, searching.

"You are wishful thinking, sir." Melwyn moved toward the parlor door, ignoring the tingle in her flesh at the timbre of that voice. She prayed she wouldn't stumble. "Do you spend the night, or take a room at the local inn where you may rape a village whore?"

"The whore sounds delectable. I need a warm form in my bed to temper the frigidness here." He sounded almost angry as he followed her back out into the hall.

"What did your daughter mean, Pencavel, that you're already married?" The widow nibbled on a chicken thigh, the conversation out here —if not the food—apparently stalled in their absence. "Aren't you a widower these many years?"

"She was distraught, Madam Whale, that's all." Her father sighed deeply. "What shall I do with her? A girl with few prospects now."

"Forgive me, Papa." Melwyn rested her hand on her parent's shoulder. "I spoke out of turn; it was nothing but chagrin at my brusque and cruel rebuff by this knave of a man." She turned to Lambrick, who watched her carefully. "Though, of course, I wholeheartedly agree with his decision." Her throat tight, she turned back to her father. "Please, don't waste your time finding me a husband. As soon as I'm one and twenty, I'd like my inheritance and will procure passage to Italy to join in the continued excavations of Pompeii and Herculaneum."

"That is preposterous! You will scandalize the region, and bring shame upon your poor father." The widow licked her greasy fingers. "Not to mention ruin your fingernails."

"I worry about your safety, my dear. I wish you would rethink this folly, though I'm under no illusion that you will," Lambrick said, his tone genuine.

"I'll be fine. Don't trouble yourself." Melwyn's words came out stilted. She moved several steps back in case he might touch her, and she'd fall into his arms.

"You've shaved years off of my life already, my girl." Papa nodded in agreement with the viscount.

"If you insist on this road to perdition, an older woman of sound character is accompanying you, I do hope?" The widow narrowed her already squinty eyes. She brushed a chicken bone from her generous bosom. "For your father's sake."

"Indeed, and this chaperone and I are very close, so no one need worry. And I will travel in disguise to preserve my father's piece of mind. I give you good evening, Madam."

Melwyn turned to Lambrick, unable to meet for long his enveloping gaze. "And *adieu* to you, Lord Lambrick. Our brief association has been

...unforgettable." She hurried toward the stairs. The deep concern in the viscount's face unsettled her. She wanted to slap and kiss him at the same time. The thought of him bedding a whore rankled her, and she wished she were insane enough to say the hell with her virtue and take a tumble with him out in the barn. But a stubborn streak prevented her from giving him the satisfaction of her body, even though he'd snuck into her soul.

Trotting up the stairs, she fought a sob as her throat thickened that she might never see him again. Clowenna stood outside her chamber door, arms crossed, a knowing—if a tad pitying—expression on her round face.

Chapter Ten

Griffin sipped from his tea, eyeing the elderly man across his five-drawer Chippendale desk in his library where shelves of books in cupboards lined the walls. Under the elegantly coffered ceiling, the smell of paper and old leather calmed him, usually. "I'd have thought you would approve of England procuring antiquities for her museums and studies here."

Sir Arthur Seworgan sipped from his own tea, the cup dangling from his bony fingers. His outmoded frockcoat was purple, long-skirted, and showed an old embroidered yellow waistcoat beneath. "I do, but I disapprove of any shenanigans over the legalities. We must always be officially authorized, and so forth."

"Of course. Do you have doubts as to my honesty, Sir Arthur?" Griffin set down his cup, wishing he had added brandy to the bland beverage. Lady Pencavel's unexpectedly upset face at their last meeting swam in the liquid's surface. He shook the vision away, nearly spilling his tea.

"I have heard, ah, rumors." The lanky man leaned forward, resembling a crow with his beaked nose and wizened face. "One does, you know. I only dig and deal in lawfully obtained works of ancient art. You are a man of, shall we intimate, shadowy reputation."

"So I've heard myself, several times." Griffin chuckled, though he was certain no mirth reached his eyes. "I keep people guessing, which I don't mind at all. But if your doubts are too severe, then I suppose we cannot discuss any business transactions." Disappointment, but not surprise, wriggled through him. Sir Arthur did have a sterling reputation.

"Good show, old bean. Distract me with a false sense of affront." The old man snickered, scratching a hand through his sparse white hair. "I only came here to warn you that the officials are circling the carriages, so to speak. They infer that you are smuggling artifacts, and that does not sit well with them."

Griffin winced at the pain in his shoulder from the bullet wound. He'd managed to escape the revenuers by sneaking into his secret passage that twisted under the ground for miles to the cellar of Merther Manor. "Then why aren't the officials here, accusing me? I'm a good friend of the sheriff, by the by."

"Friends in high places won't keep you from gaol, if you are caught red-handed, sir." Sir Arthur balanced his cup on his bony knee. "I only caution you to be aware. You are a landowner, and I know your tenants and the villagers respect you. You are generous with them, it is said. And the wench at the local tavern sings your praises to the heavens."

Griffin had kept *her* satisfied—yet he'd stayed away from her this time in his residence. He was a man of innate talents in the boudoir, if only Miss Pencavel would allow him to show her. But their relationship was at an end—he realized now he could never sully her. Heart growing heavy, he shifted in his chair and cleared his throat. "I thank you for the warning. I also have a favor to ask of you."

"Why should I grant you a favor?" The man's thin lips drooped into a frown. "You may ruin this enterprise for the rest of us honest folk. I have a standing of being a scholar and expert in the field of antiquities, and a man of impeccable character who is on the cutting edge of this new field of archeology."

"That's why I invited you here. I will invest heavily in your next excavation." Griffin leaned over his desk, luscious lips invading his mind and giving him too many sleepless nights. "I want you to travel to Langoron House near Bodmin and speak to a young woman there who is fascinated by antiquities. Treat Miss Pencavel as a serious student of the field, as she has assured me she is serious."

"A woman? That is highly irregular." Sir Arthur's mouth hung open, showing teeth that would benefit from a good scrub. "Not the done thing at all, I must say."

"As I said, treat her as a serious student. Tutor her in your field; encourage her as you would a man." Griffin turned the delicate cup in his hands, whishing it was his ex-betrothed's lithe body. "And you need have no worry about financing your next excursion."

"But a woman...I don't know." The old man scratched at his head. "They don't have the intellect to grasp the particulars that we men do."

"She might surprise you. Don't tell her I sent you, and don't waver around the more gruesome descriptions." Griffin leaned back in his chair. He could at least do this for Miss Pencavel. Perhaps the details of what really went on at a dig would deter her from putting herself in harm's way. And if not, she'd be better prepared when she did venture out. His chest constricted when he thought of her out of his reach, in Italy, among those lecherous Italians, indulging in pasta. "Do this for me and I'll also introduce you as a friend *who should be well taken care of* to that very accommodating wench at the tavern."

Sir Arthur's face split into a wide grin. "Now we're talking, old bean. I'll do what you request of me post-haste. Let's hope I can rise to both occasions."

****

Melwyn sprinkled twelve ounces of oil-soap shaved very fine into a bowl in the stillroom. "It's still four months until I'm at my majority, and it seems a lifetime away. I could be chipping at stone and earth rather than fashioning Lady Lilly's silly Soap Balls."

"Try workin' as a maid, with no husband, no children, no house of me own." Clowenna sighed dramatically as she added three ounces of spermaceti to the soap shavings.

"We'll both be adventuresome spinsters and see the wonders of the world." Melwyn made light of it. Nightly she dreamt of hot kisses, and gold buttons that pressed against her breasts, leaving sensual indents. The first thing she'd do in Italy would be to find a young Italian lover to wipe all thoughts of Lord Lambrick from her mind. She mixed in two ounces of bizmuth dissolved in rose water. She melted the mixture in the wide kitchen hearth and returned.

"Low wages, cast-off clothes," Clowenna continued as she added in one ounce of oil of thyme to the soap. "Emptyin' slop jars, a hard bed to sleep in. Bein' mistreated by your masters. *I'm just a tin miner's daughter.*"

"In Italy, I'll find us both lovers, and that will quiet you, I pray." Melwyn poured in lemon essence and oil of carraways. The light fragrance was pleasing, but she still saw her ex-betrothed's dark eyes raking over her. Her mouth went dry. She stirred the concoction, hard. "We won't be lady and servant, but only two women on a mission, to discover ancient artifacts hidden for centuries."

"We'll most likely uncover worms in the dirt." Her abigail wrinkled her nose. She started to shape the balls. "I don't care much for worms, but that's me lot."

"We'll fish with the worms, to save money on food." Melwyn tried to picture herself baiting a hook with a squiggly, squishy creature, and cringed. "Papa still hasn't said he'll give me my inheritance, but I believe he shan't deny me."

"Work your wiles on him." Clowenna slowly shaped more balls and lined them up on the still room table. "If not, we'll starve in a country where I won't know the talk o' them, since 'ee still hasn't taught me no Eyetalion."

"My lady, excuse my interruption of your rare foray into domestic endeavors, but you have a visitor." Bastian entered the still room, his head barely missing the low lintel.

"Lord Lambrick?" Melwyn said it so earnestly, the butler backed up a step. She sucked in her breath and almost squeezed flat a soapy ball. "I meant, I hope it's *not* Lord Lambrick. I despise the man."

Clowenna rolled her eyes. "No one believes that no more."

"It is an elderly gentleman. I put him in the front parlor." Bastian moved aside for his lady to pass. "Shall I bring tea?"

"I suppose. Visitors always expect tea, and any good hostess provides it, no matter the bother. Charles II's wife made tea drinking popular in England, but couldn't produce an heir, the Portuguese cow." Melwyn wiped her hands on her apron, then removed the garment, hiding her disappointment at the visitor not being Lambrick. But of course, she'd never see him again.

"Not very charitable to that long ago queen," Bastian said. "And serving tea is only a bother to the servants and kitchen staff, if I may point that out, m'lady."

"You just did, dear Bastian. Forgive my imprudent words. You like being my conscience, and I am humbled. Or as humbled as I can manage." Melwyn gave him a wry, if sad smile. "However, in Italy I'll only drink wine."

"Then we might fall in them holes 'ee be diggin' in." Clowenna started to dust the soap balls with talcum powder so they wouldn't stick together, her hands coated with soap and powder. "An', la, I'll have to climb in afore the ants eat your flesh an' heave 'ee back out. Me work is never done."

"On the other hand, I might leave Clowenna here when I sail, to soak up some of your sophistication, Bastian." Melwyn pushed her hair back into place and pondered who this elderly visitor might be. Another unwanted beau? "Serve the bohea tea, as it's cheaper than the pekoe."

She strode down the corridor and entered the parlor. A skinny old man turned to smile at her. He wore a bright blue, garishly embroidered suit with lace cuffs on his shirt sleeves. Her papa was scraping the bottom of the proverbial barrel with this suitor. "I am Lady Melwyn Pencavel. And who are you, sir? Not here for my hand, I do implore."

"I'm Sir Arthur Seworgan." He removed his fantail hat and bowed his head with its wispy white hair. "And you are no pampered princess, I'm relieved to see. There's color in your cheeks and soap muck in your hair."

"Sir Arthur Seworgan? I know about you. I've read your treatises on antiquity, digs, and keeping mosquitoes away from sensitive areas of the skin." Her heart picked up; a famous antiquarian and archeologist stood before her, though he looked as ancient as his discoveries, as if first-hand he'd witnessed the building of the pyramids. "I am elated to meet you, sir. To what do I owe this honor?"

"I cannot reveal my source, my dear, but I'm here to assist you in your studies." He seemed to force a neutral expression. "It's strange for a lovely young girl to wish it, but I hear you are interested in archeology."

"What does someone's visage have to do with interests? Despite what that overstuffed bluestocking said." Melwyn's head spun; this couldn't be happening, her dream coming true. "I'm shocked, stunned, and everything else a giddy girl—if I were one—might say. I'm dedicated in my studies and welcome your presence." She led him to the small room where she'd spread out her books, papers, quill pens, blotting sand and wax—the space her father had allowed her to utilize.

"I've been researching John Aubrey, who as I'm sure you know, was one of the first to record megalithic and field monuments here in southern England, and was the discoverer of the Avebury henge monument." She watched Sir Arthur's eyes widen in surprise. "No, I'm no pampered princess. Where do we start?"

****

Griffin held up the torch as Jacca pried open a crate lid. The dank smell of the tunnel of his underground passage pushed in on him. Roots poked in on the dark dirt walls shored up with wooden posts and bricks. Water dripped here and there in plunks. They'd at last retrieved the hidden loot and maneuvered it into the tunnel.

"Here one o' them be, sir." Jacca sat back on his heels with a grunt. "Them dirty, cracked relics from Italy."

"Excellent." Griffin leaned closer with the flickering torch, the smoky smell sharp. Three small statues, four vases, a leather bag of money. He inspected the bag's contents, the Centenionalis, Sestertius, Dupondius, a few Quinarius and a Siliqua— all ancient Roman coinage. Spearheads, terracotta pottery, bronze toga brooches were also here. "This looks like the real deal." Suddenly he thought of how excited Miss Pencavel would have been to peruse these items. But would she balk at the illegalities as Sir Arthur did? He gripped the splintered edge of the lid. "Now we must contact our buyers, and see who is interested."

"Broken pottery, ess? I has some cracked crockery at home no one would pay for," Jacca grumbled as he touched a chip on a terracotta pot. "Me old woman shied a pitcher at me head last night."

"She'll kill you some day. And that's more reason never to marry, you cranky old sod." Griffin dropped the lid and straightened. He fought a cringe at his own near brush with death. Were such precarious undertakings worth it anymore?

"At least in the grave I'll have peace from her." Jacca snorted.

"You should take her to market and sell her, as that transaction has been done before." Women, who needed them! "Leave everything here under wraps until I find a serious customer." Griffin walked, slightly stooped because of the low ceiling, back toward the steep, hidden stairs. He set the torch in its holder, ran his fingers along the rough wood until he found the hidden latch, pulled, and the door opened with a creak.

A long ago ancestor had built the tunnel, and hidden stairs, for the same purpose Griffin used it for no doubt. Griffin had played here as a boy, with his brother. They'd pretended to be pirates, how glorious the memory!

Up the stone steps, swiping at cobwebs, to another secret door, he pushed a second hidden latch, which opened into the old priest's hole, where during the break with the Catholic Church people hid their priests to worship illegally. The priest's hole was tucked behind a walnut panel and a sliding painting of Henry VIII—how ironic, the king who broke with the church in the first place so he could marry Anne Boleyn.

Griffin breathed in the fresher air when he stepped from behind the painting into his library. He poured a shot of whiskey and drank the pungent liquid, savoring the smoky, grainy flavor. He walked the room admiring his many books, the walnut woodwork, brass lamps, Turkey carpets, but yet he was here alone, with no soft arms to hold him.

He did need children, and legitimate ones, to inherit all this splendor. He must continue the ancient name of Lambrick, to honor his father. He sank into brief sadness, over his lost brother, and thinking how mildly happy his mother would have been to have grandchildren. This large house needed laughter, and grubby little fingerprints on the wainscoting.

He took another gulp of alcohol. Should he search for a meek-tempered wife, when he couldn't wipe the perfect oval countenance of Miss Pencavel, the tantalizing taste of her lips—if he could only get her to shut up—from his troubled brain?

Chapter Eleven

"I used to wander here as a child. That's when my interest for uncovering ancient secrets emerged." Melwyn stared across the sweeping vastness of the Bodmin Moor with its rocky landscape, scraggly heather, and granite tors. "My governess, a bland woman of little character, allowed me to do what I wished, which has added to my unbridled nature."

A lapwing twittered and dove through the bog moss.

"There is much to admire out here on the moor, but this is a secret of mine." Sir Arthur unlocked a gate, walked with Melwyn past high, pungent boxwood shrubs, and into a hidden garden. Past the gorse and yews, he moved aside brush, to show Melwyn a hollowed out area in the earth, surrounded by crumbling stone walls. He stumbled down and bent to sweep away the dirt from one of the walls, revealing a painted motif relating to Bacchus. "I've been excavating this villa for eight years."

"How have you kept this from other archeologists?" Melwyn's pulse soared. She stepped down into the excavation, glad she wore her leather half-boots and not silk slippers. Her fingers itched to chip away at the dirt, to reveal more of this Roman villa. "I remember trying and failing to climb over that gate as a girl. I think someone might have shot at me."

"Possibly. I call this my retreat, where I contemplate my discoveries, writings, and so on. I even have a humble cottage with thatch roof close by." He pointed to a wattle and daub structure several yards away. "No one else has seen this. People respect my solitude."

"And why do you honor me with this...great honor?" She eyed him with suspicion, as if he'd only brought her here to take advantage of her; yet she doubted he had the strength or inclination. He probably hadn't enjoyed a woman since the last Ice Age.

"Let us just say you have a benefactor, unknown to you, who insists I tutor you in this field." The old man winked. "And how could I do so without showing you my villa?"

Clowenna plodded over, holding the basket of food they'd brought. "La, why do I get stuck with such burdens? Only 'cause 'ee bein' a lady can't be alone wi' a strange man." The abigail tilted her head toward Sir Arthur. "An' he be one topper o' a strange man."

"You keep hinting at this mysterious benefactor." Melwyn plucked a leather flask from the basket and drank deep of the lemonade, the tartness refreshing, ignoring her maid's complaints. "Tell me who it is."

"He wishes to remain anonymous, my lady." Sir Arthur averted his watery gaze.

"Is it my father?" Then she was struck by an idea, suddenly, out of the blue. Her breath hitched. "It's my mother, isn't it? She's managed to elude the second under-butler, come into a fortune, and finance my interests."

"She be too busy rollin' in the hay, lovin' 'tween the sheets, and wi' who knows how many other servants by this time." Clowenna placed the basket on a Roman plinth.

"You knew her so well," Melwyn agreed, though filled with regret. It wasn't easy to have a notorious harlot for a mother. "I always hope she'll repent the error of her ways and return to us, but as Auntie says, I digress."

"Observe, my lady, down here we have red concrete floors, and below that the Romans created a complete central-heating system." He pointed out the large arched flues, the various heating channels and the vertical wall-flues. "This brilliant system kept the building warm over a thousand years ago."

"The benefactor must be my father." Melwyn smiled slyly, not believing her papa would encourage her in anything but the heavy chains of marriage. Still, she must push for details. "When I return home, I'll praise him profusely, and tell him I thanked you for telling me, yet shamed you for breaking the promise not to."

"He will pretend otherwise." Sir Arthur's cheeks flushed, bringing color to his parchment hue of a face. His hooded eyes spoke volumes. "I'd advise against it, my lady."

"'Tis Lord Lambrick!" Clowenna unwrapped a meat pie and nibbled on the crust.

"Fie! Where do you see him?" Melwyn spun around, her heart in her throat. Had he come for her? Would the viscount swoop down like a white knight on his steed and carry her off to his castle, or reasonable facsimile? She smoothed down her blue striped, risen-waist taffeta gown. "How does my hair look?"

"Naw, I meant he could be your patron, I'll be bound." Clowenna bit into an apple from the basket. "Did 'ee bring any gooseberry tarts?"

Melwyn's heart did a strange flip, but at least it had left her throat. She'd gotten what she wanted, her freedom, but why did she regret it now? "Thank goodness he's not here; I do so hate the man. His very presence would revolt me."

"Yeah, right." Clowenna snorted. "An' I'm Queen Charlotte holdin' court at Buckingham House. Georgie, the third o' 'ee, fetch me a tart."

"Well, give me that food, *Queenie*. Servants eat leftovers left by their betters, remember?" Melwyn slapped the cloth back over the victuals, crackling the basket. Her appetite had deserted her. She turned to Sir Arthur. "What century was this villa built? I know the Romans inhabited here, or dominated the ancient Britons, for about three centuries."

"The damp, dismal weather no doubt chased 'em away," Clowenna said. "It's depressing, many kill themselves."

"Go and sit under a tree and contemplate your enormous and varied sins!" Melwyn ordered, though she hated to sound abrasive to her abigail, since the low-born woman was right, she *was* the only one who put up with Melwyn's antics. "And I sincerely doubt his lordship would finance me in anything."

"Sins sounds like more fun than diggin' in the grime. An' when will 'ee, admit 'ee love that Lord Lambrick?" The maid plodded off and plopped down under an oak tree, her full brown skirts spreading out around her like a spray of dead leaves.

"If we may continue in spite of these domestic spats," Sir Arthur cleared his throat, "this villa dates back to the late first century AD."

Melwyn's cheeks burned. Why *did* she love that villain? She had no time for love. She had a life to live, and artifacts to discover. Her head swam and she nearly toppled into the deeper elevations of the excavation. Had she just admitted to actual "love?" She scarcely knew the man. Who, except in silly romantic novels, loves someone on such short acquaintance?

She grabbed Sir Arthur's fusty frockcoat front with its overlarge, tarnished silver buttons. "Take me with you to Italy. I must leave England as soon as possible."

The old man's mouth gaped, showing his yellowed teeth beneath his beak of a nose. "But you're not yet of age, my lady. Your father would have me drawn and quartered, and then perhaps even pilloried. I'm too elderly for such stratagems."

"Why must I be a certain age to obtain my independence? And even then I'd be considered property of some man, father or husband." Melwyn snatched up a brush to begin dusting aside dirt under the painting of Bacchus. An edge of something solid peeked out. She brushed harder, revealing dark blue glass. More scraping and a vase took shape. Her pulse skittered. "I believe I've found something."

Sir Arthur stared at her as if leery of coming too close again. He straightened his coat lapels. "Keep dusting, Miss Pencavel. Carry on."

She did. The dark blue vase she began to uncover depicted white figures in Roman garb, lounging under a tree. "The artifact is cameo glass, I'm sure of it." She dusted off more, then chipped around the sides with her hammer, careful not to crack the glass, and finally pulled the item out. "Behold! It's magnificent. Much like the Portland Vase at the British Museum."

"Bravo, Miss Pencavel, an extraordinary find." The old man peered closer, bushy eyebrows raised. "It's first century, confirming my estimation of the villa." Sir Arthur clapped his bony hands together.

"At last, I've made a startling discovery. I'll go down in the history books. I've read that cameo glass is difficult to come by." Her heart dancing, Melwyn traced her fingers over the opaque figures; she must travel to Italy on her birthday, and forget any foolish thoughts of men—or one grossly inappropriate man in particular.

****

Melwyn laid her chipping hammer away in its leather case, on top of her Louis XV style desk with floral marquetry and cabriolet legs. "I'll be written down in archeological magazines for my find. The Royal Society will clamber for me to join them."

"If Sir Arthur don't steal your discovery. 'Ee should o' brought that vase here an' not let him keep it at the ruin." Clowenna brushed the dirt from Melwyn's hem. "That'll need to be soaked in urine to take out them stains."

"Always the voice of doom, aren't you? But I will keep a gimlet eye on Sir Arthur." Melwyn walked to her window and swept aside the muslin curtains. The rolling green land stretched toward the sea. Her time with Sir Arthur had sped by, and the bluebells and sea pinks withered among shards of granite in the August heat. The scent of flowers mixed with the briny smell of the ocean. She recalled romping on the grounds with her governess, and wondering why she had no brothers or sisters, and why her mother spent so much time in the servants' hall.

She turned back to her maid. "I continue to ponder who this mystifying benefactor might be. Who would care so much to give me this opportunity?"

"I still say it be Lord Lambrick. He has the blunt, don't he?" Clowenna dusted rosemary into Melwyn's boots to sweeten the sweat. "An' from what I seen, he loves 'ee, as much as 'ee love him."

"Balderdash, on both counts." Melwyn twitched the curtain closed as her pulse jumped. "There is *no* love between us. And why would someone with Sir Arthur's sterling reputation deal with a man like Lambrick? I think he's a smuggler." She had eavesdropped on her aunt's and the duchess's whispers about the viscount.

"Why don't we find out, m'lady?" Clowenna shook out a chemise from Melwyn's portmanteau, her gaze alight with mischief.

"What do you mean?" Melwyn sat on her bed, hiked up her skirt and two petticoats, and untied her gold filigree silk garters from above her knees.

"I mean, 'ee need some adventure afore you leave England. Still over two weeks till you're of age, an' no promise o' money to sail. We could travel to that there Merther Manor an' see what the man be up to." Her abigail sat beside her. "I could question his servants, now couldn't I?"

"That sounds foolhardy to the extreme." Melwyn rolled down her stockings, her mind tumbling over this suggestion. The possibilities of seeing Lambrick again did entice yet unnerved her. "Why would I care to be anywhere near that blackguard, in his own home, under his jurisdiction?"

"To uncover the true criminal that he be?" Clowenna poked her shoulder with a forefinger. "'Ee could snoop about that huge manor 'ee refuses to be mistress of. No secret your da controls your inheritance. If we prove his lordship be a miscreant, it might shock the master into givin' 'ee control. How else is we to live abroad?"

"You are a conniving wench, whom I've taught well. But—it still sounds insane." Melwyn rubbed a cramp in her calf from her climbing about the villa. "Lord Lambrick might never allow us to stay there, and would mistrust our motives." The remembrance of intense dark eyes sent shivers along her shoulders. She sighed. "Dash it all, I like it. We'll do just that, and I am curious about the manor. I'll send a letter announcing our impending visit, but we'll leave here before he'll have the chance to refuse us."

****

Griffin stared across into the pasture at his flock. The sheep were Dartmoor, a descendent of Cornish Heath. Medium sized and short legged, the animals were classified as Lustre and Longwool. They were shorn now, and looked bedraggled as they munched at the grass.

He smiled in appreciation that their wool financed his other activities and the upkeep of his home.

He breathed deeply of the mossy smell of the pasture, the stink of sheep. Then the scent of linseed oil reached him, and he turned. Mrs. Loveday, his housekeeper, approached.

"Good afternoon, sir." The slender older woman with the pert face smiled her sweet smile he remembered from throughout his life. "They're fine specimens, your sheep."

"Indeed they are. The estate is well managed as when my parents were alive, don't you agree?" Here was one woman whose approval he'd always sought.

"It is. But when will you wed, sir? You need a fine lad to leave this estate to. Don't let it pass to a greedy cousin, or some-such nonsense." She tugged at her mobcap lappet. "Since your beloved brother died in the war with those frog-eaters, there is no heir."

Griffin stuffed aside the mention of Alan. He loathed to think about his younger brother who died in the Austrian Netherlands, fighting the damned French. His stomach clenched. This tragedy gnawed at him, but it was best to leave the past in the past.

"You ask me about my marriage prospects every day. Before, I could put it off, but I am rethinking that decision as I am growing older." He should pursue a docile, insipid girl, but the idea made him downhearted. For some reason, the blistering spirit of Miss Pencavel was much more to his liking. However, he had little hope of ever taming such a hellion into a recognizable domestic pattern.

"Your dear, if very ordinary parents, would have been exceedingly pleased to see you happily settled, sir." Mrs. Loveday patted his shoulder. "And perhaps it is time to curtail your dealings—though I know nothing about them—in your secret tunnel."

"It may be time to desist, if I'm not yet certain. A woman would heartily disapprove, as you've just proven." He turned around to view his home. Built in the Elizabethan era, where comfort took place over defense in more peaceable times, Merther Manor was constructed in an H shape with tall many-paned mullioned windows in its golden brick facade. The roofline was curved in a Flemish influence. "I released Lady Pencavel from our contract, and I'm sure she was delighted."

"You were always a wayward boy, but this may be for the best, m'lord." Mrs. Loveday lowered her eyes. "If I may speak out of turn, you do know about her mother?"

"A shame that the poor girl must live under such a dark shadow. However, I didn't think it common knowledge. Most of the *ton* in London seemed ignorant." He harbored sympathy for Miss Pencavel? Griffin shrugged it off. He must move on, trudge forward, march into battle...philosophically of course.

"She isn't good enough for you, sir. Inclinations like that could run rampant in the blood." The older woman shook her head in lament. "The servants wouldn't be safe."

"Lady Pencavel professed a clean slate to me." Nevertheless, women could find many ways in which to finagle.

A horse galloped in the distance. When horse and rider drew closer, Griffin stiffened as he recognized the sheriff of the Padstow region.

Rawlyn Tremayne reined in his mount, and lifted his bicorn hat. "Good day to you, Grif. Mrs. Loveday, it's always a pleasure."

"Is it a pleasure, Raw? What brings you out to my estate?" Griffin considered the sheriff a friend, but any lawman on his property presented a problem. "Do I have poachers?"

"We're the profoundly honest people we've always been." Mrs. Loveday smiled benevolently at the sheriff. "Nothing to see here." She excused herself and scurried back into the manor.

"Merely a social call, pray?" Griffin asked, studying his friend. "I have some fine Canary we could partake of, if you are so inclined."

"Don't I wish, my good sir." Raw dismounted and swiped his hat over his dusty breeches. "I'm afraid I've had more complaints from the excise men, and because of that, the High Sheriff is concerned." His horse snorted and stomped a front hoof as if in agreement.

"In what capacity are these unfounded complaints, exactly?" Griffin turned from the man to hide any guilt, and started to walk toward the elegant, studded front door of his home.

"The revenuers say they were here about three months ago, and almost caught smugglers down in the cove." The slender sheriff followed, his gaze noncommittal, his boots scuffing the gravel drive. "They're certain they shot one of them."

"Is there a body somewhere in the cove I should know about?" Griffin did his best arched-brow-in-irony as he paused before his door. He twisted at the front latch. "It would be decomposed by now."

"Wounded, only, I believe." Raw looked him up and down, and up again, his brow now arched as well. "How is your health?"

"Couldn't be better, thank you for asking." Griffin's shoulder had completely healed by this time. He refrained from touching it. "If this incident happened months ago, why are you questioning me about it now?"

"I put if off for as long as possible, but pressure is being applied." Rawlyn shrugged, but it seemed in exasperation. "I do have a job to perform, no matter our relationship."

"I understand your unenviable position." Griffin had behaved himself these past months, hoping everything would quiet down—or perhaps just slowing down himself. He disliked putting his friend in such quandary. "What else is the High Sheriff, the redoubtable John Enys, concerned about?"

"That a man of good lineage and huge property holdings could be delving into illegal deeds." Rawlyn stood, arms akimbo, scrutinizing Griffin. "I've warned you before, Grif. Soon I'll be forced to act."

"I pay my taxes on time, finance a war I wish had never happened, and have never sired any by-blows—that I'm aware of." Griffin gave his what he knew to be disarming smile. He pressed a knuckle into the knot of tension on his nape. "He should leave me to my own devices."

"A lawless land is not to Mr. Enys's liking." Rawlyn crimped his thin lips. "Don't force me to investigate you too closely. Why must you play the daredevil? Find more acceptable pursuits."

"Acceptable as the rest of my class? Drinking myself dotty on port? Gambling away my fortune, perchance? Dying in a duel over a perceived insult?" Griffin leaned against his door, his jaw tight. "I invest my money into the people here, my tenants, that's what drives me." And the thrill of being devious and clever, he didn't say.

However, he was starting to admit to himself that his nocturnal exploits didn't hold the same incentive as they did before he'd met a certain golden-haired vixen.

****

The hired landau driver hurried his team along the road to Merther Manor under scattered oak and beech trees. "You ladies without male escorts, tisk, tisk; wouldn't have happened in my youth," the middle-aged man grumbled. "'Tis not safe at all."

"Don't be nettlesome, sir. Why do we women have to be treated like children?" Melwyn swayed in the seat and smacked his shoulder with her glove. "Women have sought rights to no avail for centuries. Christine de Pizan in the fifteenth century defended the value of women in her, *The Book of the City of Ladies*. And Englishwoman Aphra Behn was an abolitionist and a spy for Charles II. She also wrote plays deriding forced marriages."

"Me da was right; they should never teach women to read—or write, God preserve us." The driver slapped the long reins over the horses' sweaty backs. "Preggers an' barefoot, that's the way to keep 'em."

"I'm still waitin' to be taught." Clowenna glared at her mistress as they jostled along. The silk flower on her straw hat bobbed up and down with the vehicle. "All this talk o' women's rights, an' where's mine?"

"We'll start in the morning with your ABC's and P's and Q's." Melwyn nearly fell off the seat at the next jolt. She grabbed the wrist strap. "My dearly appreciated but impatient maid."

"Criminey, what's this world come to? Teachin' lowly *servants* to read and write?" The driver groaned then spit out onto the road. "You should be whipped, Miss. You are not natural."

"And you are an impertinent bounder. Do you realize you are speaking to an earl's daughter?" Melwyn had never hidden behind her father's rank before, but couldn't resist the opportunity. Her stomach roiled at the ride, and the idea that any moment she'd reach Merther Manor. "I'll have you know that in 1696, that's a *hundred* years ago for an oaf such as you, sir, reformer Mary Astell wrote a thesis called *A Serious Proposal to the Ladies*. Her astute observations stated that the male patriarchic system was responsible for the differences between men and women. Education, or the lack of it for women, was the signature factor in this issue."

"Oh, la, here we go; she's off on a tangent." Clowenna pulled her hat brim low as if she could pretend she was invisible. "I shoulda listened to me mam and become a laundress."

"So, in conclusion, saying I'm not natural, or *not* a woman of my time, is ridiculous and flawed." Melwyn sat straighter and stared out from the open landau. Astell also warned against attraction being a factor in marriage, when understanding should prevail.

A long drive through spreading oaks led past a well-scythed lawn. A brown hare raced across the path, ears twitching, then disappeared into the ferns.

Around the next bend, an H-shaped Elizabethan manor came into view. The afternoon sun glistened off its honey-hued facade and curved gables, and shone off the many-paned windows, turning them to diamonds.

Melwyn leaned out from the carriage and gasped. "A magnificent place, I must admit. Too bad its owner is such a scalawag."

"We has no proof o' that yet." Clowenna swiped dust from her face. "That's why we're here, m'lady."

The landau bowled up the gravel drive. Under the manor's front portico stood two men, one tall and lean, the other shorter and quite slender.

Melwyn's pulse hammered when she saw the taller of them was Lord Lambrick. She was definitely attracted, but understanding him seemed beyond the pale.

The driver reined in his team, hopped down and started to unload the women's luggage.

Melwyn alighted, straightened her clothing and straw hat, and swiped a tendril of hair behind her ear.

Lambrick glared over, then strode toward them, his gaze thunderous. "What is this, Miss Pencavel? I was not expecting a visit from you."

"'Tis a whole lotta trouble, if you ask me," the driver muttered. "The pretty one has too much brains in her head. And the muffin-faced one is set to rise above her place. I'm havin' fits, I am."

Melwyn sauntered closer, her flesh heating at beholding again the viscount's handsome visage. Danger exuded from him. "You didn't receive my letter? I do apologize. I thought I'd drop in and be neighborly, since we were almost related to one another, through a disastrous but thankfully cancelled betrothal."

Lambrick strutted up to her, and whispered, "Since you deem it 'thankfully' cancelled, then you have no reason to be here. You are tempting fate, and me. What is your ploy, Miss Pencavel?"

His warm breath on her cheek made her shiver. He was correct, she was tempting fate to put herself this close to him, but she couldn't back down now. Risk and daring were part of her makeup. Ever since her mother had abandoned her, she was convinced that life was "anything goes." She had managed to hold onto her morals as far as sexual misconduct was concerned. So far, anyway.

"Will you invite me in, or be cruel and send me away?" She made her voice demure and watched him from under her lashes. "We are quite exhausted and need a good wash, and an offer of food wouldn't be unwelcome."

"Please, you must introduce me, Grif...that is, Lord Lambrick." The thin man joined them, the gaze in his narrow face assessing. He grinned, stretching his suntanned cheeks wide. "To this very lovely lady."

"Sheriff Tremayne, this is Lady Pencavel. A tentative, sort of—the jury is still out— friend of mine," Lambrick spoke through stiff lips. "I must have forgotten about her, ah, visit."

"Good to meet you, my lady." The sheriff bowed and tipped his cocked hat. "I'll be on my way now, Grif. Remember, people are watching, so have a care. I beg of you." The man mounted a horse and rode off in a surge of gravel.

Lambrick opened his front door, gesturing for Melwyn to enter. He sent out two footmen to haul in the luggage, and Clowenna. Melwyn walked into a cool, spacious entrance hall with an ornate plaster ceiling that soared like froth above her head.

"What did the sheriff mean by 'people are watching'?" She waved her gloves between them as she stepped across the black and white checkerboard marble floor.

"That's none of your concern, my dear, so keep your pretty nose out of it." He put his hand on her arm, and she nearly jumped out of her skin. Why did his touch affect her so? He smelled like grass, sheep and infinite peril—if peril could have a scent.

She moved away from him in her swirling rose velvet traveling dress with short jacket. She twirled the matching riband on her hat. "Does he speak of me, being here, vulnerable, with no chaperone?"

"No, not at all, though your reputation will be under scrutiny. However, it's been questionable for a few years, at your own doing. Your travels about the county with just your abigail—such as today, haven't gone unnoticed." He thrust his hands behind his back as if to resist further touching. "Shall I have my housekeeper show you to a room? Or are you here to share mine?"

"As usual you overstep yourself, sir. I will not be compromised. My travels were always of a business nature, even if that shocks your male sensibility." She stared at a naked statue in an alcove, her mouth dry, her stays growing too tight. She'd made a huge mistake in coming here; she couldn't deny that she wanted this devil's spawn, though aloud she'd deny it vociferously. Taking a slow breath, she faced him. "Call your housekeeper before you say anything you, or I—or anyone else in our vicinity—may regret."

Chapter Twelve

"Deuce it all, just what I need, that barbed-mouthed brat under my roof. Why is she here? What does she want, after so brazenly rejecting me before I had the chance to reject her?" Griffin gulped his brandy in the library, the smoky, smooth taste not quite soothing down his throat.

"'Ee covet the chit, don't deny it, sir." Jacca bent over a tally book on the large desk. "Your smitten face tells it all."

"I won't deny it, yet smitten is too harsh a word. But to *have* her is to marry her in our society. And neither of us wishes marriage, even if I need it to pass along my prestigious name." Griffin rubbed his face in confusion, and he disliked being confused and not in total control. He'd been with his share of women, and enjoyed their favors; however, none had captured his heart, or lingered in his thoughts after the relationships ended. "I'll need to find a compliant, dull wife, set her to breeding, and neglect her because she'll bore me."

"Sounds like the perfect plan." Jacca dipped his quill in ink and scribbled more numbers. "Should o' done that meself."

"A man should be able to have two wives, one for respectability, and one for titillation." Griffin poured himself another brandy from his cut-crystal decanter.

"That's what a mistress be for, sir." Jacca dusted sand over the page to dry the ink. His craggy face crinkled further. "If I was ever so lucky to have one, me harridan of an old lady would kill me if I enjoyed meself."

"Regrettably, I don't want a mistress anymore. I desire the unpredictable Miss Pencavel. And she's already turned me down for an illicit tryst, at least twice." Griffin hoped it was only desire he felt for her, and not something more treacherous...like love. He shuddered at the thought. To love such a brash, untamable creature was opening himself up to disaster and discontent. He gulped more brandy. Her intractable nature was what attracted him to her; she was a lot like him—yet he couldn't be in love with himself! Or could he?

"Find out why she's here, sir." Jacca put the quill in its leather holder and wiped ink-stained fingers on a cloth. "Maybe she's changed her mind about the tryst."

"I plan to, as soon as I finish this alcohol. I need a little Dutch courage." Griffin tipped up the snifter and upended the beverage, which burned down to his stomach. "I've always been the most courageous, some would say reckless, of men. How dare this wisp of a girl presume to transform me."

"Looks like she already has," Jacca replied sagely.

Griffin slammed down the snifter. "We'll just see about that." He left the library and stormed up the stairs, and down the long gallery of elegantly paneled wood, past solemn portraits of upstanding Lambrick ancestors. He knocked on the guest-chamber door.

The moon-faced maid opened it, her gaze wary. "Might I help 'ee, your lordship?"

He rocked on his heels. "I will speak to your mistress at once."

"She's in slight dishabille at the moment. Could 'ee come back later, sir?" The maid started to close the door. "Or tomorrow would be better."

"At the risk of being a rude host, I will speak to her now." He pushed open the door and was caught up in the sweet fragrance of lemon, not to mention the enticing view of Miss Pencavel in a flowing pink, silk dressing gown, her blonde hair in disarray over her shoulders.

"You are an insistent fiend, aren't you, my lord?" She pulled her robe close, even if her eyes glinted in amusement. "Have I no privacy?"

"Not when you invade my household with no prior notice." He stepped into the room, his pulse thrumming. "I want to know exactly why you are here."

"A reasonable request, I will admit, even if I did send a missive in the mail. You cannot trust mail service these days." She ran her fingers through her tresses. "And since I have ostensibly invaded, I won't stand on ceremony." She sashayed closer. "I'm here to find out who you really are."

"A very dangerous prospect, my lady." His stomach tightened, with her too near body, hidden badly in the flimsy garment, *and* the idea she might discover his secret operations. "Since we are no longer betrothed, why is that of interest to you?"

"I am a woman who does not mince words, I find you enigmatic and therefore fascinating." Her perfect eyebrows rose as she appeared surprised by her own admission. "An *unfortunate* prospect, on my part."

"She's that stubborn, an' in love wi' 'ee, milord." The maid smirked and exited quickly through the connecting door.

"My abigail exaggerates, of course." Miss Pencavel's cheeks flushed scarlet and she turned her back to him. "Disregard what she said, and even what I just said. I'm overtired from the journey."

Could this little minx love him? His chest heated with the oddest feeling. It must be the brandy. "Are you here to reinstate our association, Miss Pencavel?" To his shock, the idea didn't revolt him as it once might have.

"That's the silliest thing I've ever heard. We're both free to do what we want. Well, you much more than I." She walked away, her form outlined alluringly in the silk. "I can tell you have no care for me, as you keep mentioning my less than pure reputation. Is that why you rejected me?"

"You are a confounding creature. You sought the dissolution of our contract as well as I." Griffin bristled, irritated at the sympathy that rose inside him. He wanted to embrace her, to press her silken body against his hard-muscled frame. "Aren't we both satisfied with the outcome?"

"I daresay we are." She gave him a drained smile. "It was a moment of madness for me to come here. Do forgive me."

"No, I apologize for my boorish behavior. I shouldn't have barged in on you just now." Griffin went to the door; he had to leave, to collect himself, to wipe her scent from his nostrils. "I will see you later, for supper, where I hope you'll have more clothes on."

Back in the corridor, he marveled at their polite banter. He'd spent many years perfecting his impervious exterior, to not plunge the depths of his loneliness. He could not allow this young woman to unmask him—nevertheless, he'd still enjoy her in his bed.

****

Melwyn entered the adjoining room and threw a brush, purposely badly aimed, toward her abigail's head. It thwacked on the wall behind her. "I should thrash you, which I am allowed to do. But I feel for you as a woman stuck in a degrading profession. Why *did* you say that I love him, you tattling slyboots?"

"Because 'ee do, that's all, m'lady." Clowenna picked up the brush and plucked out a loose bristle. "Look, the ivory be chipped."

"And my papa says *I* don't know how to dissemble. Of course, I did just admit to Lord Lambrick I was here to find out who he is." Melwyn flopped down on the maid's hard, narrow bed. "I should never have allowed you to talk me into coming to Merther Manor. Did you see the way he looks at me? First, as if he could strangle me, then a minute ago as if he might gobble me up for pleasure."

"Ess?" Clowenna tossed the brush on the bed, opened her sewing basket and began to thread a needle. "He loves 'ee, too, but won't admit it neither. You're both mulish blockheads an' must know how the story will end."

"What does it matter? The situation is impossible. If we did marry, which we won't, we'd tear each other apart like two angry bears being baited. He'd never allow me to pursue my interests. And...I seriously doubt he loves me." Heart heavy, she shifted on the straw mattress, relieved hers was of soft feathers. "Anyway, I will sail to Italy, and drag you and now Sir Arthur with me, if he can survive the voyage."

"Only if your papa gives 'ee your money." Clowenna sat in a chair, pulled out a black, woolen stocking, and began to thrust her needle in and out, mending a tear.

"Very well, we are here. So as soon as it's dark, we'll sneak about the house and find out if his lordship is smuggling." Melwyn smiled hesitantly, back to her original purpose. "We need to search for secret passageways. Smugglers always have them in their homes."

"An' hope it will scare your papa into givin' 'ee your portion, no strings attached." Her maid's needle continued to swipe in and out of the material as she deftly stitched.

"That sounds preposterous, and a contrived plot-point, now that I ponder it, but we'll carry through with our plans." Melwyn stood, shoving any thoughts that she could love a crook and *he* might love her far away. The smuggling aspect didn't bother her, but the idea that this man had such sway over her emotions did. "Lay out my darkest dress, and wear yours; we must creep like phantoms through the house."

Hours later, after pleading illness to keep from attending supper with Lord Lambrick, Melwyn opened a tinderbox, struck steel to flint, and lit a pilchard-oil lamp. Dressed in her dark blue dress, she and Clowenna crept along the corridor.

"Did you find out anything from the servants while eating in the servants' hall?" Melwyn waved the stink of the fish oil from her face as she whispered.

"Ess. A footman told me to look in the library for a secret passage." Clowenna inched along in her dark bed gown, the loose wrap worn by servants.

"That sounds far too accommodating on such short acquaintance." Melwyn stopped at the head of the stairs and scanned the area. Her skin prickled with nervousness.

"I spoke to the only surly servant who don't like it here, cause the others raved about the benevolence o' the viscount. His handsome an' burly valet worships him." Clowenna smiled then shrugged. "But there's always one malcontent in the bunch."

"Brilliant. I hope you obtained directions to this library." After instructions, Melwyn started down the stairs, cringing if one creaked, her maid on her heels.

Thunder rumbled outside, and rain began to splatter on the manor roof.

"It would rain," Clowenna said in a tense whisper, "Now it'll feel all spooky."

"Is there something you need, Lady Pencavel?" The housekeeper loomed out of the gloom like a spider, her question almost an indictment. "A tincture, since you aren't feeling well? Or so you said."

Melwyn jumped, wriggling the lamp's flame. She steadied her breathing. "I need fresh air, a short walk; that will revive me." This woman had been churlish from the start, as if Lambrick were her son and not her employer. "It's nothing to trouble yourself with, Mrs. ...Loveday, was it?"

"Yes, it's Mrs. Loveday, trusted keeper of the peace and linen at Merther Manor since his lordship was a child." The housekeeper raised her pert chin and scraped suspicions eyes—fine wrinkles pronounced in the shadows—over Melwyn. "Shall I accompany you on your late night promenade, my lady? Bring you an umbrella, perhaps?"

"I have my dear abigail with me, so no need to bother." Melwyn raised her chin in her finest earl's daughter pose—she could duel chins with the best of them. "I adore the rain. So please retire at once."

The woman glared her up and down. She twisted at her mobcap lappet. "I'm well aware of who your mother is. Do you need directions to the servants' hall?"

Melwyn swallowed a retort. She must maintain an even temper as she was prowling around someone else's home. "No, I most resolutely do not. Goodnight."

"I will retire, with one eye open, you may be assured." Mrs. Loveday grasped her skirt and mounted the stairs ever so slowly.

Melwyn waited until the footsteps in the gallery above faded. She blew out her breath. "Strident old biddy. If I was mistress here, I'd have her sacked."

"'Ee still has the chance," Clowenna reminded. More rain pounded on the roof.

Down another gloomy corridor, Melwyn and her abigail entered a large room that smelled of leather and smoke. The light from the lamp barely touched on the numerous shelves of books. A large walnut desk, a smaller neoclassical desk by Maggiolini, and leather chairs filled out the area.

"Run your hands along the books, to try to find a latch or lever of some type," Melwyn whispered, the lamp flame flickering in her gush.

"I'm doin' it, over here in the dark in case 'ee hasn't noticed," Clowenna groused. "Keep your knickers on, m'lady."

"We don't wear knickers yet." Melwyn traced her fingers along the smooth and tooled leather volumes. "Though why is beyond me, and it's extremely inconvenient at times." She felt along the shelves, frustrated that she found nothing.

"I don't feel naught but books an' more books. Who has time for so much readin'?" Clowenna grumbled, then the sound of tripping and a thud. "La, and damme, I walked into a picture frame."

"Shhhh. Do you want the wrath of his lordship, or his dragon of a housekeeper down on us?" Melwyn hurried to where she stood, shining light over the maid who rubbed her nose, and a tall portrait of Henry VIII that hadn't swung on the picture rail. "This seems solidly in place."

Melwyn pushed on the frame and the picture slid to her left. "Oh, my, I think we've found it." She shone the lamplight on a dark wood panel.

"How do we open it?" Clowenna sniffed loudly, still intent on her nose.

"Find a latch or lever." Melwyn handed her maid the lamp, and felt along the panel's grooves and carvings, her fingers dipping into every nook and cranny. Finally, something metallic under her fingertips. She lifted it, and the panel creaked open slowly.

Melwyn grabbed the lamp and shone the light inside a musty, tiny room. "It looks like a priest's hole. There is even a cabinet where they hid the sacred vessels and vestments."

"Hope there's no dead priest in there." Clowenna gripped her mistress's shoulder.

"I thought you weren't a superstitious ninny." Melwyn stepped in, and soon discovered another latch. The far door squeaked open. The dank smell of earth swept in on her, almost dousing the lamp. "This must be the secret tunnel."

"Great, we found it. Now we can go home and tell your father." Clowenna tugged on Melwyn's arm. "I'm tired; let's go up to bed afore we're murdered."

"I remind you that this was your idea." Melwyn shook her off and put one foot into the tunnel, her heart racing. She held up the lamp. "This could be a passageway built by a previous ancestor and have nothing to do with Lord Lambrick."

"That be wishful thinking, m'lady." The maid tapped her foot in irritation. "Now come back an' don't do no too-stupid-to-live act."

"We need more proof," Melwyn insisted. She chewed on her lower lip. "How will I take you to the continent if you're going to be a nervous Nellie?"

The light barely reached down the tunnel with its crude shored-up walls, and the sound of water could be heard farther along. Melwyn shivered in the cooler air. A stack of crates sat a few yards away. She walked toward them, and reached out her hand to touch the top one's scarred lid.

A shadow moved to her right. A hand grabbed her wrist and she gulped in astonishment, almost dropping the lamp.

Chapter Thirteen

Griffin wanted to jerk her arm from its socket. He'd waited around, hunkered down in his tunnel, suspicious of her reasons for visiting. "Too sick to share supper with me, my lady?" He pulled her close, her blue eyes wide in the lamplight. "Just what do you think you're doing down here?"

"I'm snooping, exactly what it looks like I must admit, sir." Miss Pencavel tilted up her nose in defiance, even as her pretty mouth trembled.

"And are you satisfied with what you've discovered?" He leaned even closer, until their noses almost touched. She smelled divine.

"You have an intriguing tunnel, and you're aware I love digging." She smiled, but it looked forced. The mellow light, despite the off-putting fishy scent, danced along her soft cheeks.

"There are no Roman ruins down here, my lady." He gripped her arm harder then regretted it when she flinched. "Is this why you came here, to reveal my private business?"

"I intimated as much earlier." She tugged at her arm. "You're hurting my wrist, sir."

"I'd like to hurt far more, most of which you wouldn't understand if your claim at remaining virginal is true; but I demand to know your intentions." He released her, his threat inexplicably warming him inside.

She rubbed her flesh. "I was under the idiotic misconception that if I could prove you a deviant of some sort, that my father would rue the betrothal and give me my inheritance."

"Was this hare-brained scheme yours? I expected more from you." He scowled, then followed her gaze to the maid who held back, acting nonchalant, whistling an off-key tune. "You're here because your *maid* thought it was a bright idea to intrude on my affairs? I've already denounced the betrothal, so what madness is this?"

"I truly wanted to see your lovely home." Miss Pencavel stared down the tunnel. Tendrils of her hair curled in the damp air around her delicate ear. "Very well, my curiosity and stubbornness got the best of me. Is this why you don't wish to marry, because of your smuggling? Did you think I would disapprove and turn you in?"

"You have proof of nothing, other than I have a tunnel under my manor house. I appear to suffer from very large gophers." He tried to relax his tense muscles, and not reach out to touch her ear. "You are trespassing, and I insist we return upstairs."

"I would not turn you over to the law if I was—and thank goodness I'm not—your wife. I'd only worry that you'd be sent to gaol." She faced him again, her mouth obstinate, but looking so soft and sensuous, like rose petals. "Now what will you do to me?"

"I should beat you, but we're not married as you stated." He chuckled dryly but couldn't resist tracing his fingers along her smooth cheeks and jaw. His body hardened in places he wished it wouldn't. Why did she stir him so? It could only be unrequited lust.

"Usually when you accost me, you kiss me, roughly and thoroughly—as insulting as that is." She narrowed her eyes, but made no move to leave.

"I'd rather kiss my pipe-puffing bailiff." Of course, that was a lie. He wanted more than anything to kiss her, but refused to give in to the emotion, furious at finding her down here. He pulled back his hands and waved one toward the door. "After you, my lady. I think you and your reprobate of a maid should depart for Langoron House tomorrow."

"I might need longer to rest; I don't yet know. We women are prone to the vapors." She still didn't move, her gaze questioning. "Did you send Sir Arthur Seworgan to me?"

Griffin sighed in vexation. He nudged the nosey maid into the priest's hole and shut the door, leaving him alone in the tunnel with Miss Pencavel. Dark shadows draped like a cloak around them. "I've changed my mind. I will kiss you, and meticulously."

He jerked her against his chest, his lips seeking hers in hot abandon. Desire thrummed through his loins as her lips responded in kind. She tasted like honey. She set aside the lamp, or he did, and trailed her fingers through his hair. He roamed his hands along her hip, up her back and deliciously close to her breasts. She moaned and wiggled into his hips.

Then he groaned and pulled away, ever so reluctantly. His heart pounded like a drum roll. Never before had he wanted a woman so badly. "Am I still correct in assuming you continue to refuse to spend the night with me?"

"Of course I still refuse," she gasped and fanned herself with her hand, "I'm a decent woman, in that aspect at least."

Griffin snatched her up and tossed her over his shoulder. She was light, but wriggled fervently. He strode past the maid, through the library and up the stairs. In the guest chamber he dropped her on the bed.

"You ghastly beast," she sputtered. "You've upset my equilibrium, and my stomach."

"If I were a beast, I'd take you right here, and as rough as possible." He hovered over her, tempted to do just that, but he needed no more complications in his feelings for this hoyden. "Don't move, or I'll rip off your bodice and teach you things that would astound you."

"You wouldn't dare! This is imported silk." She scooted up higher on the mattress, her hands flying to her inviting neckline, her cheeks flushed. "Why *do* you keep kissing me like a man hopelessly enamored?"

"How many others have kissed you in such a way?" he growled, struggling to restrain his pulsing loins. He hated to ponder the truth of her statement.

"Not a one; but I have read a few novels on the subject, when I wished to waste my time on frivolous pursuits." She brushed a finger over her swollen lips and eyed him slyly.

Griffin stifled another groan and went to the door. He had to get her away from him, out of his hair and out of his blood. "*I'll* give you the money to travel to Italy, along with this Sir Arthur person who I've never heard of before. Pack and head for Plymouth in the morning. You can take a boat from there to Dover, then on to Lisbon, and Italy after that."

"You believe I'll refuse, don't you?" She knotted the counterpane—the punctured silk quilt his mother had lovingly sewn—in her fist. "But I won't. By the time I reach Pompeii, I will be one and twenty. I accept your offer."

"Good. And I hope you grow up while you're tramping about in the heat." Her resolve made his heart do an odd twitch. "Wear sensible shoes and a wide-brimmed hat, my lady."

"If growing up means giving in to the bullying tactics of men, then you wait in vain, sir." She said it softly. "A strong woman is always viewed as hysterical or unladylike," she spouted as he shut her door.

Griffin rushed to his own chamber, shed his frock coat, waist coat and shirt. Pouring water into the bowl at his wash stand, he splashed the tepid liquid on his heated face and chest. Water ran in rivulets down his muscled abdomen.

"Can I be of assistance, sir?" Kenver rushed in wearing his nightshirt and nightcap. "Are you all right? I heard sighs of morose discontent."

"I'm fine as can be managed at this interval, my good man; go back to bed." Griffin ran both hands through his damp hair.

With Miss Pencavel out of England, he could go back to his normal life, raising sheep, and enjoying his brandy—and maybe just one more time smuggling artifacts. He'd search for a pasty-faced, dim-witted heiress as soon as possible to beget his needed successor.

****

The stark white cliffs loomed up out their inn window. Melwyn stared out at the shingle beach where little boats were drawn up, and larger ships anchored farther away bobbed in the channel. Her tormented thoughts bobbed about as well. "We're finally here, at the edge of England. So close yet so far, as I'm philosophically expounding."

"Do as 'ee will, but this bed be full o' vermin, m'lady," Clowenna said as she swiped aside dingy sheets. "We'll need to get some oil o' tansy. Even the common likes o' me won't sleep in 'em."

"I wrote Sir Arthur. I hope he arrives soon." Melwyn turned back to the shabby little room. She fought a disappointed moan. "The air is fetid in here. Let's walk out into the town and make that purchase of tansy."

She wore a plain, closed-robe, dull brown dress. She'd pretend to be a widow as previously stated, her husband killed in the war. The two women pinned on their straw hats with small ribbons and left the inn.

The sharp wind off the channel cut into her and Melwyn pulled her cloak close. Dover was a jumble of narrow, winding lanes, crowded with overhanging buildings and stinking cow pens. They passed numerous leering sailors as they made their way to the market square.

"How do we know we won't be killed by blood-thirsty rebel French soldiers?" Clowenna asked.

"We don't. I suppose that's part of the adventure." Melwyn spotted an apothecary shop and they entered to the tinkle of a bell. She should be excited that her journey was beginning, but she missed the livid voice and chastising eyes of Lord Lambrick. She tried not to dwell on the fact she'd taken his money for this expedition. She'd find a way to pay him back.

The shop's spicy smells was a relief from the stink of sea and seamen.

A woman strolled toward them slowly. She was tall and slender, with a vaguely familiar face. Her yellow, low-cut gown sans scarf seemed out of place in this establishment, the style incongruous for the middle-aged clerk. "Good afternoon. May I help you ladies?"

The elegant—and bored—voice struck an uncomfortable chord in Melwyn's memory. "Pardon me, as I am candid, but I seem to have met you be—"

"Oh, triple la!" Clowenna's hand flew to her throat. "It be your mam, in the unholy flesh, as I live an' choke on the shock."

"Don't be impertinent, Clowie," Melwyn scolded, stunned, unbelieving, even slightly disgusted. "This is a terrible mistake, obviously."

"Melwyn?" The woman narrowed her eyes a little—as if surveying undercooked mutton. Her eyes were the same azure blue as Melwyn's. Her tone remained languid. "Can it possibly be you? How very perplexing."

"Since that is my name, and it's unusual, it *must* be me." Melwyn's heart clenched as her fingers shook.

This woman before her, an older, more drawn, version of herself, was actually her errant mother? She could barely form the next words. "Have you lived in Dover all this time? With that wretch of a second under-butler?"

"In one way or another. Such a tedious city, but here I am." The former Lady Pencavel raised her chin. "Nonetheless, men come and they go, in the grand scheme of life."

"Still shameless, ess? My, not-so-much a lady." Clowenna stared from her to Melwyn. "Bold as brass, like your daughter; though *she's* kept her virtue, far as I know."

"I'm nothing like my mother. Go and look among the bottles for what we need." Melwyn pushed her abigail—none too gently—toward the shelves of jars and bottles along the wall to distract her repugnance.

"How is your father? Is he still alive?" her mother asked in a voice devoid of emotion. She made no move to embrace her only child, and Melwyn was strangely grateful there wouldn't be a false scene of a happy reunion.

"He was devastated by your departure." Melwyn paced about the shop, repressing her anger. She inspected the fluted blue bottles and ceramic jars of the apothecary trade. "But I'm certain that was secondary to your desires."

"You had no idea what I endured in my marriage." The woman averted her gaze, trailing a hand along her salaciously revealed cleavage.

"But what about me? Didn't I deserve a letter now and then? A gift at New Year?" Despite herself, Melwyn's throat thickened. She hadn't expected to confront her mother, ever, and had no armor—or spear—for this unexpected meeting.

"I thought you better left alone." Madam Pencavel shrugged a shoulder. "What I did was scandalous by the standards of the day, and you should be grateful that the stain of it didn't fall upon you."

"You're wrong, it did." Melwyn's reply came out staccato sharp. "Papa pretends you're dead, but many know the truth."

"Wait until you're suffocated in a dreary marriage. And your husband expects you to be faithful to him—every day." Her mother leaned against a cupboard with small drawers where seeds were probably stored, acting as if they spoke about the price of tea in China. "You'll seek out the occasional bootblack and groom to brighten your moments."

"You should have been honored to share the ancient name of Pencavel," Melwyn protested, mortified by her mother's words.

"The name means 'horse-head' in Cornish." Madam tilted her head flippantly.

"Be that as it may, I never intend to marry." Melwyn fought a quiver, remembering Lord Lambrick's strong shoulder digging into her diaphragm as he carried her up the stairs. "You must never have loved Papa or me, but did you love the under-butler?"

"*Second* under-butler," her mother corrected with a raised finger. "The first under-butler was too religious for my tastes. All those sermons during our trysts, as if we weren't already tempting hell."

Melwyn squeezed her eyes shut. The fact her mother was so immoral validated her resentment. She stared again at this woman who birthed her. "You *are* unrepentant. I don't remember you ever being affectionate to me, merely shuffling me off to various nurses and governesses."

"Too busy givin' 'affection,' or at least her favors, elsewhere, it be evident," Clowenna mumbled as she clinked among the bottles.

"Are you happy here?" Melwyn asked, gazing around the snug little shop. Her hackles up, she wanted to hear that her mother was miserable, atoning for her sins. "Are you keeping company with an apothecary now?"

"What is happiness? A fleeting feeling of carnal satisfaction. My attentions always wander." Her mother flicked a finger over a carboy. "I've only been in this shop for a week, and I'm already bored, though the young apothecary clerk looks appealing."

"You lack true feeling for anyone. I see that now." Melwyn took a deep, cleansing breath, even as tears gathered at the back of her eyes. "My poor, dear Papa. How he's suffered."

"I was forced into that marriage against my will." Madam shrugged again. "My father thought it better if I married quickly, after that incident with our steward."

"How do you not have a flock of children by all these liaisons?" A disturbing thought occurred to Melwyn. "How do I know Papa *is* my father?"

"There are herbal remedies to prevent conception, my girl. A smart woman knows how to use them, and when. Queen Anne's Lace seeds are the best." Her mother patted a seed drawer then scrutinized her. "I so wanted a boy, such a pity."

"I'm letting go of my feelings for you, to alleviate myself, *not* to exonerate you. You are not worthy of me or my father." Melwyn stifled more vitriol. She would encourage her papa to shed his delusion and begin the expensive process of divorce. She turned to her abigail. "Did you find the tansy, Clowenna? I'm ready to leave."

"I'll give you the family discount," her mother said with a wry smile.

Back outside, Melwyn shoved her coin purse back into her reticule. A sob with a scream attached threatened to burst forth from her. "I must never think of that soulless woman again."

"She's a piece o' work, isn't she?" Clowenna shook her head. "An' I thought me mam, who ran a brothel, were bad."

"I admit I have the odd thoughts and escapades, but I've always retained my chastity." Melwyn stalked along the twisting lane, lifting her hem from the muck. "If I find someone to surrender it to, it will be for love, but never marriage. I'll never have casual, perfunctory affairs."

"'Ee need his lordship." Clowenna grinned when Melwyn glowered at her. "After we go to Italy, o' course. But 'ee know once your reputation, even if 'ee never done nothing, only the *appearance* o' impropriety, be damaged, 'tis hard to recover it."

"I'm well aware of that ludicrous reasoning. And mine is already tainted, by my own actions, and those of that distasteful woman I won't mention." Melwyn stepped over a drunken sailor lying in the road. She resisted kicking him—because it wasn't his fault Madame Pencavel had scoured her nerves. She hurried toward the inn. "Did you hear what that person formally- known-as-my-mother said? She used the words 'dreary' and 'tedious.' That sounds like me, lamenting my situation. I must *never* do that again." Melwyn stood tall, shoulders squared. "I'm now the Widow Byrd, because I'm free as a bird. And you're my faithful companion, Mrs...what *is* your last name?"

Clowenna grimaced. "It be Buckett."

"Really? How ill-fated. As is 'horse-head' I suppose. And your mother actually ran a brothel? I do pray that you weren't ill-used. My poor excuse for a mother probably recommended you for my maid." Melwyn pulled open the inn door, her head full of differing emotions. "Well, I'm glad of *that* at least. Widow Byrd and Mrs. Buckett will soon be off to Italy and fame and fortune."

Chapter Fourteen

In sleep, Griffin tossed and turned, then flipped in the sheets on his four poster bed. Blue eyes and a mocking laugh disturbed his dreams. He reached out his hand to touch her face, half-wanting to strangle her instead. He moaned and squeezed his down pillow. Then brown eyes that matched his own replaced the blue. He saw his own cocky smile, no, only similar. His brother Alan stood before him, youthful, and vibrantly alive.

"What ails you, Griffin? You look like you've swallowed too much of Godfrey's Cordial." Alan repositioned the arrow in the nock of his bow. The cool breeze over the field ruffled his blond hair. The shadow of Merther Manor stretched behind them.

"Well, I am in dire pain. It's your commission into the army that troubles me. We'll soon be at war with France, I've little doubt, after their overthrow of their king, heads on bloody pikes, and all that followed." Griffin's anger coated over his fear. "Father wants you to go into the church. You should have persevered with that calling."

"Father means well, but has no imagination. The clergy vocation is too tame for the likes of me, and you know it. We are both rebels, dear brother." Alan drew back his arrow and released it. The point found its place in the target with a thud. "What a great sport, catering to society's tastes for the gothic and medieval."

A footman rushed forward and pulled the arrow out, then ducked out of harm's way.

"You don't think you're too old to go? What do you know about the military? Are you going to throw Bibles at the enemy?" Griffin stroked the sleek yew wood of his bow.

At four and twenty, his brother had entered then left seminary school, and shocked the family when he'd asked their father to purchase a commission with the 8892nd and Two-Thirds Regiment.

"Very droll. I'll hobble on crutches and creaking knees to my fate. But I'll exchange a Bible for a musket." Alan laughed. His handsome face lit up. His slender body looked muscled in his white breeches and fine Holland shirt. He'd flirted with many a willing young lady, but never became serious with any of them. A tendency shared with Griffin.

"Not amusing. What if anything happened to me? You are the spare heir." Griffin cringed inside at the thought he could lose his only sibling. He nocked his arrow, gripped the bow in his left hand, pointed his left shoulder at the target, and pulled back the bowstring with his right fingers. The tension of the gut bowstring, his tightening arm muscles, redirected his disturbance. The arrow sliced through the air and also hit the bull's eye with a thwack.

The footman dashed over the scythed grass and retrieved again. The autumn air rustled the crimson and golden leaves above their heads, the breeze mossy with dying foliage.

"Never fear, Grif, the Lambrick brothers are invincible." Alan winked, nocked another arrow and shot once more. This time he was slightly off center. "Ah, we may have lost our colonies, but such sport proves England's unity, greatness and patriotism, and other such blather."

"And our exclusion of the middling class in our archery clubs, to also prove our worth in the aristocracy." Griffin chuckled sardonically. Then he frowned. "Are you doing this to prove your worth since you probably won't become viscount?" The idea pierced him inside. "I won't be the catalyst for such foolhardiness."

"I suppose I needed a challenging purpose, and preaching to the parishioners, begging for tithes, and eating supper with people I don't like—who would probably not be able to afford the food and fine wine I prefer—didn't hold the same thrill. Besides, moldy churches make me cough." Alan ran his hand through his hair, reminding Griffin of himself. His brother turned his gaze on him. "Marry a sweet heiress, father children, and get on with your life."

"Does the heiress need to be sweet? I might like a girl with a little fire and bite. A woman of substance to heat up my bed." Griffin laughed too loudly. He hadn't yet made up his mind to the sort of woman he would want to be his wife—easier to ignore what society deemed as inevitable for a future viscount. Then he stepped closer to Alan. He wanted to smell the familiar scent of their youth, the stables, the cricket field, the shearing shed, now, even in his dream, knowing it fleeting.

"I'd advise you to quit your more dangerous pursuits." Alan stared toward the cove, his expression growing serious, then his features appeared to melt like hot wax. "Which one of us will be shot first?"

"It's too *late* for that, don't you understand?" Griffin almost shouted. He reached out to touch Alan, but his brother started to fade, like smoke in the wind. Griffin's hands grasped nothing until he felt an item, soft and pliable.

He awoke with a jerk, clutching his pillow against his heaving chest.

****

Clowenna leaned over the rail of the two-masted, square-rigged, packet boat, again losing her lunch in the slurping waves that bashed the hull.

"Perhaps we should have hired a coach for this leg of our journey," Sir Arthur said. The old antiquarian looked a little green around the gills as well. The wind rippled the lace around his scrawny throat.

"A coach would have taken forever through Portugal, Spain, skirting through France, then into Italy, not to mention the danger, in the middle of skirmishes and battles." Melwyn rubbed her own stomach as the boat rocked. She held tight to the rail as sea spray sprinkled her flushed face. Would they ever reach shore? She was sick of the stink of brine and mildew. She'd paid a high price for her freedom, but hated to complain aloud. "Soon we'll be immersed in relics and ancient dust."

Sails loomed up near the horizon; a ship bobbed on the choppy Mediterranean Sea that appeared to stretch on forever.

A sailor on their ship raised his spyglass and scrutinized the vessel. "Ship ahoy! She looks Frenchie, Captain! A 74-gunner, I believe!"

"Oh, la, we'll languish in a French dungeon, we will," Clowenna cried as she swiped her kerchief across her mouth. "We'll die in the Bastille!"

"The Bastille was torn down at the beginning of their revolution." Melwyn's heart thumped and she stood on tiptoe to study the ship. Her abigail's melodramatic behavior and illness unsettled her further. "Be brave, Mrs. Bucket."

The sailors swarmed the rigging, rearranging the sails. Shouts permeated the air.

The captain, a stout man of middle years, stepped to Melwyn's side. "Mrs. Byrd, we'll attempt to outrun that ship. We're too small to engage her."

"Oh, dear, I'm too old for this falderal. I should have insisted on staying in England." Sir Arthur checked his pulse, his large nose bobbing like a toucan. "I hope my affairs are in order."

"Are we fast enough to outrun her?" Melwyn asked; a sudden excitement seized her. She held on to her fluttering hat, its riband whipping against her back. "We must be, having fewer cannon to weight us down."

"We shall see. You and your party should go below." The captain tipped his salt-encrusted hat brim and left them.

"I'm not hiding below. This is what I came for, adventure! I want to feel the burn! And live life to the fullest!" Melwyn laughed, her mind on this, and not her other issues and heartbreak. Sir Arthur and Clowenna eyed her in trepidation.

"I must protest, my lady, and insist that you come below with me." The old man clasped her arm. "I'd prefer drowning to being blown to bits by cannon shot, so to speak."

The packet's sails billowed with wind, the rigging creaking, the ship lurching as it cut through the water. The French warship sailed closer, tall and menacing.

"I'm perfectly capable of making my own decisions, sir." Melwyn shook him off and gripped the rail with both hands, the spray dampening her hair and cheeks. Her pulse raced. She couldn't drown now, not after traveling this far, and deserting Lord Lambrick for good. "I will ride this out like a carved figurehead. A mythical being reminiscent of Minerva."

"She's lost her mind, I fear." Clowenna groaned. "An' I only lost me biscuits."

A shot fired from the warship. The cannon ball splashed into the water, thankfully far short of their vessel.

Melwyn froze, having second thoughts about this particular adventure. Her knuckles white on the rail, she hated to lose face and retreat. Her tiny cabin was like a rollicking box, portending death.

She turned to her right, and swore she saw land in the distance. Her feet slipped an inch on the slick deck. "Land ahoy! Over there! I see it!" she shouted, before the sailor in the crow's nest had the chance. He spewed a salty expletive at her.

"We're saved, thank the good Lord." Sir Arthur raised his bony arms to the sky. "However, do forgive me for long neglecting my faith, and so forth."

A rocky coast appeared, dotted with a few shrubs. Olive trees and junipers grew higher on the slopes. The smell of earth and plants was heavenly.

"Italy, at last!" Melwyn sighed as their vessel slipped into a cove, evading the warship in tall reeds. She sagged in relief against the hard teak rail. "We are meant to be here. To forge on, successfully." Fate was not against her, she would prevail. "Something incredible awaits me, I'm certain of it." Her anxious proclamations eased her frazzled nerves. Prying her fingers loose from the rail, she knew she'd behaved very imprudently just now, and regretted it—a little.

"Include me in your big event, so I can survive." Clowenna sucked in her breath, her wide brow furrowed. "That be too close. I'm about to lose me supper, an' I hasn't eaten it yet."

"You are always included, my weak-stomached companion. We're on to Pompeii." Melwyn laughed, this time not like an idiot. She embraced her abigail, but dark sensual eyes in the corner of her thoughts reprimanded her unruliness.

Chapter Fifteen

Griffin stood in the former solar of Merther Manor and forced a polite smile at the pretty-enough young woman before him. "I appreciate you coming to call on me today. We might get to know one another better. What do you do for pleasure, Miss Trefoile?"

"I'm honored to be invited, sir. I embroider not too badly. And I paint, but it's a bit mediocre. I play the pianoforte, with average skill I've been told." She fluttered her stumpy eyelashes, her light brown eyes devoid of spark, as dull as watered down broth.

"And what is your opinion of the economic crisis or the war?" He took a sip of the too-sweet sherry as the girl's parents watched from the other side of the room. He expected nothing profound on these topics, but he hoped against hope.

"Oh, I have no opinion. No one usually cares what I think on such lofty subjects." She giggled and it raked like spikes along his spine. "My father warns me not to ponder anything too deeply."

Could he suffer years of being wed to such a twit? Yet this is what he sought, a slow-witted girl from a respected family on which to father an heir—despite his recent declaration in that disconcerting dream he'd tried to forget. Her large dowry was also of value, but he hated to think of himself as mercenary, and he didn't need the money.

"Indeed." He rolled his shoulders to ease the tension there, taking another quick sip of sherry to numb his frustration. "I suppose you've been trained exclusively in the running of a household and a large staff of servants?"

"I hope so. I am a muddle-head at math, and I never could master any other language, except English." She hunched her shoulders in her ivory-colored, round gown, the hue doing nothing for her too-pale skin. Her dark red hair was also unfashionable by the current standards. The girl had been shown at a few Seasons with no takers, and was no longer in the first bloom of youth at five and twenty. Although alabaster skin was a sign of the aristocracy, she could use some time in the sun.

"Isn't this marvelous; I have such expectations." Mrs. Trefoile smiled broadly, as if already redecorating the room and reordering Griffin's life.

"I pray we aren't here on a fool's errand. I won't have my girl played false." Mr. Trefoile nodded his pudgy face, his eyes flinty. He rubbed his paunch.

"And what are your views on marriage and husbands?" Griffin asked the daughter. He had invited the Trefoiles here to force himself into making a commitment, and they were close neighbors. Still, they hadn't spent much time together, and Miss Trefoile was usually in her schoolroom—learning little as it turned out.

"Oh, that I'm to be an obedient wife, and do whatever my husband wishes." She grinned with too much gum and he cringed.

"I once wished for a woman like that as well, but now I see the idiocy of my ways," Griffin whispered to himself.

The mischievous eyes and lively smiles of Miss Pencavel crept in and he wondered how she fared in Italy. Sir Arthur had promised to keep him informed, since it was Griffin's money, and for no other reason.

"A faring, sir? Baked fresh moments ago." Mrs. Loveday proffered a tray of biscuits. She smiled knowingly. "I hope everything goes well. You are such a nice, suitable, young lady, Miss Trefoile."

"Oh, thank you. You are too kind." The girl giggled like a silly goose again.

"Subtle, as usual, Mrs. Loveday." Griffin picked up a biscuit and bit into it, the ginger taste tangy and rich. "I do like spice better than bland, unfortunately."

"Bland is easier on the stomach, and easier to manage. Perfect for a man of...particular activities and proclivities, sir." His housekeeper nodded and carried the tray over to the Trefoiles. "Unlike another peppery, foul pot of stew I won't mention."

"If you want to wallow in monotony, and though I know you care about me, you don't always know what's perfect for my singular tastes." Griffin glared after his housekeeper, then looked down again at Miss Trefoil. He had no desire whatsoever for her, and realized, suddenly, it would be as unfair to her as it was to him, to bind her to a husband that would only use her for cold breeding. Even if many marriages were contracted in this fashion, it was not for him.

"What are we discoursing about?" Miss Trefoile gave him another of her vapid smiles. "I'm completely lost."

"Indeed you are, my dear. Have you ever heard of Pompeii?" he asked, certain of her ignorance. A streak of warmth threaded through him at his new design.

"Is it some sort of hair tonic?" She flushed, but it didn't improve her pasty skin.

"No, it's a place I've always wanted to travel to, war or no war." He gave her a swift bow. "If you'll excuse me, and do forgive me if I've given you or your family the wrong impression, but I have plans to make."

He strode from the room, his graciousness shocking him. That Pencavel minx had burrowed under his skin, changing him into someone he no longer recognized. But now he didn't mind the transformation.

****

Melwyn swiped sweat from her forehead and kicked pumice dust from her half boots as they walked down the cobbled Consular Way. "It's a shame that the previous king of Naples had most of the artifacts stolen for his own aggrandizement."

"The spoiling of Pompeii has gone on for too long." Sir Arthur hobbled beside her, his lace cuffs flapping. "Wall paintings and pottery were destroyed in the first unplanned excavations decades past, until scholars—such as I—complained."

"Are 'ee certain that volcano won't erupt again, buryin' us alive?" Clowenna, aka Mrs. Buckett, held on to her hat brim, the blue ribbon waving in the brief hot breeze. She glared over at the formation in question that thrust up like a thumb in the distance.

"There's no certainty when it comes to volcanoes." Sir Arthur coughed loudly, rubbing his back. "I'm getting too old for this, I fear. And with the French and Austrians fighting in and around Tuscany, I don't feel safe."

"Italy does have a much more sultry sun than England, even in September. And I'm sick of hearing about this war. Let the French have their revolution—as long as they don't fire at me again." Melwyn wiped grit from her eyes, praying the soldiers wouldn't bother with Pompeii. She didn't want her first official dig interrupted. "Over here, I read they've uncovered the Theatre area, the Triangular Forum and the Temple of Isis." She walked toward the massive columns that looked baked reddish-brown in the unyielding sun. The volcanic dust swirled around her feet. The light smell of verbena and lemon carried on the air.

"Why do we care how these people lived? If all the good items was pilfered, why bother?" Clowenna sat on a plinth, a basket in her lap. "Me feet ache like the devil."

"There is still so much to uncover. An entire, bustling city was blanketed over in 79 A.D. Many undetected treasures await." Melwyn studied the architecture, her heart thrumming at being here and involved. The only sour note was, she expected Lord

Lambrick to rise out of the dust at every turn, perhaps dressed as a gladiator.

"Now, my dear, why are you masquerading as a widow? You didn't by any chance marry and lose a husband while you were at Merther Manor?" Sir Arthur mopped his brow and studied her with his myopic eyes.

"No, banns must be called for three consecutive Sundays before anyone can marry. I wasn't away that long." She swatted aside a fly, and banished Lord Lambrick looming over her, threatening to rip her bodice, from her memory—however, inside she twinged. "I need the widowed status for propriety, although I detest propriety since it's too limiting. Let's move on."

"I wondered why you didn't wear black. Very well. Over this way then. We are in luck that this new king Ferdinand IV, and his wife, encourage the better managed excavations." Sir Arthur fanned his handkerchief in front of his face, his beak of a nose beet red. "Their director of archaeological works, Francesco La Vega, champions the cause."

"So I have him to thank for me blisters? Where's a chariot when I need one?" Clowenna dug around in the basket and pulled out a flask. She drank deeply, then passed the leather receptacle to Melwyn.

"Aren't I supposed to drink first, you gluttonous harpy?" Melwyn sighed, giving up hope of ever changing her abigail. She sipped the cool punch, savoring the delicious and new flavor of pomegranate. "That's just what I needed."

"Over there they've began to uncover the *Via delle Tombe* with the *Villa di Diomede*." Sir Arthur waved his damp handkerchief in that direction. "This huge villa was built with staggered floors."

"Did everyone live in villa's? Where'd the poor folk live?" Clowenna asked.

"No one cared about the poor, sadly enough." Melwyn approached the Villa of Diomedes on the south side of the *Via dei Sepolcri*. She walked up the steps to the entrance, which opened onto a peristyle, or courtyard. She found shade in the shadow of the colonnade and swiped damp tendrils of hair from her cheeks with the back of her hand.

Clowenna heaved up the basket and followed with a heavy sigh. "This not be as excitin' as 'ee led me to believe. Never thought I'd miss the rains o' Cornwall."

"The villa is thought to be the house of Arrius Diomedes, a freedman," Sir Arthur stared balefully at the maid, "because it's situated opposite his tomb."

"The place has unusual architecture, with its use of space and light." Melwyn picked her way across the courtyard, over dust and weeds then past a stone plunge bath. Where would be the perfect spot to look for forgotten artifacts?

"Careful, my dear. It's still dangerous to walk around in there." Sir Arthur staggered along the way she'd come, his blue, scrolled stockings already gray with grime. His black leather shoes with red heels were woefully inadequate for this venture.

"Don't worry, I'm fine. I left my *father* in England, sir, remember. Don't mollycoddle me." Melwyn stepped over a paving stone, tripped on a broken one, and suddenly, her feet felt sucked in. She tumbled, elbows and knees striking earth and rocks. She covered her face, sliding down in an avalanche of dirt. She now grappled to stop her fall, her fingers scraping at loose earth. Feet kicking, she struck a stone floor, and landed with a thump on her backside.

Her ankle throbbing with pain, not to mention her bum, she swept dirt from her face and hair. She coughed to clear her throat and struggled to catch her breath. Using the kerchief about her neck to swipe grime from her eyes, she stared around as the air cleared.

Debris fell from above, pinging on her head. "Are you all right, Miss Pen, uh, I mean Widow Byrd?" Sir Arthur's anxious voice called out.

"I...don't know yet." Melwyn flexed her hands and arms, where scratches stung. Her elbows smarted. "Don't move up there, you're making more dirt trickle in."

"I need to go find some help; oh dear, very dangerous as I warned." The old man moaned. "I'll just crawl backward, don't wish to bury you further, and fetch someone."

"Oh, la, I knew she'd fall in a hole!" Clowenna cried. "Is she dead? The master will have me head, he will. Bloody hell. I'll miss her."

"I'm *not* dead! And watch your mouth. You sound more and more like a niggling crone as you age." Melwyn struggled to stand in the shadowed chamber. Her knees ached, stockings torn, and her skirt was ripped. She could barely put any weight on her left foot.

The only light sifted through the hole she just tumbled from, casting a shaft of brightness over a mosaic tile floor. She brushed aside dust to reveal a depiction of warriors in blue and white tile wrestling with a bull.

The musty-smelling chamber looked like a bathing room, with a huge communal bath cut into the floor. Strange paintings of people decorated a wall, above nooks that were probably used for clothing storage. She limped closer, wincing. "I wish I had a lantern." The figures' shapes and limbs seemed all over the place. Then heat infused Melwyn's cheeks. This was one of those erotic paintings famously unearthed in the city.

In the corner, where someone must have stashed them in a hurry, was a jumble of items. Dragging herself over, she saw bronze statues—she had excellent eyesight even in the gloom—gold and emerald necklaces, and blue glass vases. "Oh my! A veritable treasure trove!"

Her head felt dizzy and she dropped to the floor again, rubbing her temples. The shadows closed in around her, her ankle swelled, and she prayed Sir Arthur found help quickly.

"But at least I've made another startling discovery." She sighed, the sound echoing around her. "I'll miss Clowie, too, and Papa, of course; I hope he doesn't marry the Widow Whale—an atrociously manipulating woman. And perhaps I'll even miss Lord Lambrick; I suppose I do love him in my own odd way. All right, *I do,* deeply! And why do people talk to themselves when they're alone? I best shut up now to conserve my energy." She wiped the taste of pumice and volcanic ash from her mouth. Her body shook with apprehension. "But I'll be brave, entombed with my bounty."

Chapter Sixteen

Griffin removed his frock coat and wrapped the rope around his waist, his anger prickling across his shoulders along with the heat. "How could you have let her go off alone like that? I told you explicitly to watch over her."

"I was right behind her, and she's not a child, though many men treat women like they are." Sir Arthur slumped on the front steps of the Villa of Diomedes. His bottle-green frock coat and orange velvet breeches were covered in dust. "She's quite a determined and intelligent young lady; and if you haven't noticed, she does what she wishes."

"I have noticed, never doubt that. I'm well aware of the propensities of that stubborn miss. Luckily I found you at the right moment, barely off the boat from that dreaded country filled with those evil frog-eaters." Griffin hefted Sir Arthur to his feet and they crossed the courtyard. His worry for Miss Pencavel stunned him, tightening his stomach. "Now you say the ground is unstable over here?"

"Very, do be careful." The old man held his handkerchief to his large nose. "I wish I had the agility to assist you."

"Oh, sir, please rescue her." The maid sat near the hole, her round face drooping, her pale-as-straw hair matted. "I been tryin' to talk to her, to keep her spirits up, but she tol' me to shut me gob."

Griffin kneeled close to the gaping orifice, trying not to dislodge anymore dirt. "Miss Pencavel, it's Griffin Lambrick. Are you all right? Well, of course you aren't as you're stuck down a hole, but..." He cocked his ear to listen, but heard nothing. His heart constricted. "I'm coming down. If you're near the opening, please move back."

Kenver, his valet, held the other end of the rope in his muscled hands as Griffin inched his way through the crumbling earth, then slipped down as more dirt scattered. He coughed in the dust and held on as he was lowered, the hemp cutting into his flesh. His booted feet touched solid ground and he squinted around him.

In the dim light he saw a figure slumped next to a wall. He hurried to her, and touched her shoulder, caressing the back of her neck. His fears stabbed through him. "My dearest Miss Pencavel. Are you injured?"

"An ancient Roman, or are you Isis? No, she's a woman." She raised her head. Her voice sounded raspy. "Now I know I'm dreaming. Lord Lambrick, you cannot be here."

"Look at the fine mess you've got yourself into, my dear. Are you hurt anywhere?" He wanted to hold her close, but instead he scanned her scraped hands and torn clothing. Then he glanced up at the wall, at the erotic paintings with ancient fertility gods cavorting. "You've had interesting art to look at, however."

"More interesting than I could have imagined." She laughed wearily. "My ankle is swollen, perhaps sprained. Are you wearing a gladiator outfit, perchance?"

"Not at the moment, my lovely earl's daughter." He raised an eyebrow, then pulled a small silver flask from his waistcoat pocket and opened it. He tenderly wiped dirt from her mouth. "Here, sip this brandy. The alcohol will perk you up."

She took a sip and coughed. "I'm perked up, thank you. I'm beginning to think you're real. Too bad about the outfit; I think you'd look well in one."

"I'm quite real and confounded in my concern for one naughty chit of a woman." He replaced the flask, realizing he thought of her *as* a woman and not simply a girl. He slipped one arm under her knees and the other around her back and lifted her up. Her body shifted warm against his.

"Wait, over in that corner. There's jewelry, statues and more." She waved a sluggish arm.

Was she delusional? Griffin fought the urge to investigate, but he needed to get her to the surface and a surgeon. "I think you dreamt that, my dear. Put it from your mind." His fingers flexed against her pliant flesh. He barely stopped himself from kissing her sweet, upturned lips. He'd send a footman down into this cave to investigate later.

****

Griffin paced the inn's corridor outside of Miss Pencavel's room, his chest afire with anguish. If anything happened to her, he'd be devastated.

"So you're certain there was nothing of value down in that hole?" Sir Arthur asked for the fifth time. The old man looked like a skinned chicken with his freshly washed, sunburned face and big proboscis. "Perhaps it was merely too dark to see anything, old bean."

Griffin struggled with his conscience, surprised he still had one where artifacts were concerned. "I saw only rubble, damaged walls, shards of glass, and so forth." He had to think this out further, wait for his footman to report back. Teeth gritted, he'd then decide what to do, smuggle the booty out or inform the correct authorities. But his fears for Miss Pencavel were paramount.

The door opened, and Mrs. Buckett—as the maid insisted on being addressed—poked out her head. "The surgeon be finished, sir. 'Ee may see her now, if 'ee still wish to. Or be on your way, your choice. If I had me way, I'd say to cuddle up to her."

"I wish to see her, thank you very much. However, alone, if you don't mind, Sir Arthur?" Griffin entered the room where an Italian doctor was buckling up his case.

Miss Pencavel lay in the bed, covers pulled to her chest. She thanked the man for his service and the laudanum in perfect Italian. The surgeon bowed to her, to Griffin, and left.

"My reckless Miss Pencavel." Griffin pulled a chair over to the bed and sat. She smelled of rose water, and not volcanic ash, now, her hair brushed back neatly from her high, scratched forehead. He ached to touch her.

"You were quite the gladiator, sir." She smiled at him, her eyes sleepy. "But why are you in Italy?"

"I like to travel and hunt beautiful, exotic animals. How is your ankle? Not broken, I hope." He couldn't—and wouldn't—tell her how much her smile meant. He gripped his knee.

"No, only a sprain. The pain is lessening." Her near dreamy voice slid like melted butter over his skin.

"The drug, no doubt. I daresay you'll know better than to traipse around excavations again." He gave her his most charming smile, chasing away his urge to kiss her. "And I will return you to England."

"Oh, you are so wrong." She scooted up in the bed, then grimaced. "After what I discovered, I'll be famous, and with any luck accepted by the male archeologists as an equal."

He had scant hope of discouraging her—and found he didn't want to (he had sent her Sir Arthur)—but he remained torn about the artifacts. "Please, tell no one about what you saw, not yet. Thieves abound, and you don't know whom you can trust."

"I haven't said a word, except to you." Her voice sounded groggy now. Her slim white neck was exposed above a silky nightgown, and it drew him like a moth to a flame. "Can I trust you not to diminish my finds, or to claim them as your own?"

"I promise I won't diminish your finds." He resisted trailing a finger across the top of her breasts. But could he make that promise? He might convince her she'd imagined it all, but that sent a twinge of regret through him. He reached for her hand and gently squeezed it. "Rest, and we'll talk later, my dear."

She stretched out on the pillows again. "We're so polite to one another now, it's hard to fathom." She closed her eyes, then opened one of them. "I do think you're following me, still."

"I am a bounder of the worst sort, as you well know. Sleep, my lady. I'm relieved you are all right." He stood and called for the maid, anxious to leave so she wouldn't see anything poignant on his face. Why couldn't he admit his affection for her? He'd come all this way.

""'Ee are a fine gent for savin' her, if do say so, your lordship." Mrs. Buckett tucked in her mistress and flashed him a quick smile. "She be so pig-headed, she don't always know what's best for her."

"That makes two of us, we're an incendiary combination." He put on his cocked hat and returned to the corridor, confused over the supposed treasure, but more so, confused about his feelings for Miss Pencavel. He loved her, of that he was pretty certain, but should they have an affair—if she allowed it—or throw in the proverbial towel and marry? But would she consent to marriage when she'd sworn she wouldn't?

His throat went dry as a desert as his heart danced, waltzed and minueted, at the idea of loving her. Nevertheless, what sort of husband would he make attached to such a bold female?

****

Melwyn sipped the last of her chicken broth, hot in her stomach. "He acted overly concerned for me, did he?" She stretched out her sore ankle on the mattress and winced.

"Ess. An' very tender his lordship was." Clowenna grinned as she handed her a cup of chocolate. "He gazed upon 'ee most sweetly, even though 'ee was a mess."

"I do remember, down in the bathing room, his great solicitousness." She sighed, recalling how he held her, the warmth and security of his arms. She also remembered the treasures she'd discovered. Would Lord Lambrick plunder them, and smuggle them to England—if that's what he was doing, as she still had no irrefutable evidence. "I'm certain he followed me to Pompeii, but for what purpose? He couldn't know I'd find anything, which I haven't."

"To see to your wellbein', o' course." Clowenna fluffed out the bed curtains. "His valet told me that his lordship was tryin' to court a local heiress, but balked at her flightiness an' sailed for here."

Jealously at this news pricked her. Melwyn had come to expect him showing up, following her, disrupting her plans. How could he do that with a wife in tow? She drank of the nourishing chocolate, the bitter cocoa flavor so rich, to hide her sinking of the spirit. She wanted him, yet didn't want any man to be her master. "I can't stay in bed much longer. I'm dying of boredom—at the risk of sounding like that person who used to be my mother."

After a knock on the door, Sir Arthur entered, appearing bent and fatigued. Huger bags had formed under his eyes. His garish clothes were rumpled, and why mix purple with orange? Melwyn should introduce him to Aunt Hedra as they shared the same lack-of-fashion sense.

"Feeling better, my dear?" the old man asked in fatherly tones. "I will never forgive myself for what happened. Not the done thing to allow—"

"It was my fault and not yours, sir. I am much better." Melwyn set down her cup. "Have you been out to the site?"

"I have, and the oddest thing. There are guards at the hole." He shook his sparsely-haired head. "They won't allow me near it."

"The Italian authorities?" Her heart lurched. They would steal her thunder, confiscate her cache, ruin her chance at immortality. But in reality, she had to admit it was their treasure first. "Fie! How did they find out? You didn't report anything, did you, Sir Arthur?"

"No, no, why report a hole? I was concerned for safety reasons, until I saw the guards. But these men looked English to me, and the one who warned me away sounded like he was from Cheapside, not Naples." Sir Arthur twisted his three-cornered hat in his hands. "Very perturbing and highly irregular."

"It might be Lord Lambrick's doing." Melwyn sucked in her breath. She glanced up at the antiquarian sheepishly. "Why would he guard a place of little, in fact *no* significance? I must be mistaken."

"I asked his lordship, but he denied any involvement." The old man slid away his gaze and twitched at the lace on his sleeve.

Melwyn decided to be firm. "How long have you known Lord Lambrick? He wouldn't be my benefactor, would he?"

"What has he told you?" Now the old scholar looked crafty, eyes hooded. "Or, ah, I don't know of what you speak."

"They know each other well," Clowenna confirmed as she rearranged a ribbon on a hat, as she'd become adept at tying the now trendy large bows. "I asked the valet. He has such elegant speech. Servants know everythin', the quality not much. We should be in charge. We don't pussy-foot about."

"You certainly seem overly friendly with this valet," Melwyn snapped, annoyed that Clowenna fished out the information before her. Yet her body heated, gratified that Lambrick thought enough of her to offer Sir Arthur's expertise. "I thank you, Sir Arthur, for all you've taught me, and for journeying to Pompeii with me. I realize I can be...extremely enthusiastic in my pursuits."

"That be a nice way o' puttin' it." Clowenna picked up the chocolate cup.

"I admire your talents, and persistence, my dear." The old scholar sensed his dismissal. He bowed. "I give you good day, Lady Pencavel, and wishes for a swift recovery." He plopped on his hat, dented with finger marks. "But I can't help thinking I'm being duped about the hole."

After the door shut, Melwyn turned to her abigail. "Go out at once and find me a walking stick, and whatever serves for a hackney here. We're hobbling back to the ruins." Perhaps, she'd also find the enigmatic viscount at the villa.

****

Melwyn faced the first guard in the dusty peristyle. Her ankle throbbed and she leaned on her walking stick. The fresh air was a reprieve from her humid chamber. "Who is employing you, young man?" Though the man was probably older than she was.

"I cannot say, Miss, sorry. I have orders to follow." He was definitely Cheapside.

"This is my dig, and I demand some answers. Has anyone gone down into the hole?"

She straightened, giving him her best I'm-far-above-you-and-in-charge look.

"I employ him, my lady." Lambrick's strong voice from behind sent shivers along her nape. "I thought you would be pleased that your excavation was safe."

She turned, her breath sharp. "I am, but I wonder at your motives, sir."

"Why would you doubt me?" He half-smiled and stepped close, towering over her. "Have I not proven myself to you yet?"

"That would take days to reply to." She smiled slowly, gazing into his dark eyes. He sparked urges in her she had no idea she possessed, a warm, extraordinary tingling. "Given the gossip about you, and what I discovered at your estate, I should have misgivings."

"Are we back to sparring, my lady? If we are, I have many more years of experience at it than you do." He said it as a challenge, his eyes glinting.

A warm breeze blew up, sending dead leaves skirling across the ancient cobbles.

"You seem to doubt my equalness to the task." She said it softly and twisted at the gold button on his frock coat. "I'm disappointed, as you should never underestimate me."

"Believe me, you never cease to enthrall me, and I'm a difficult man to enthrall." He assisted her behind a large column, out of sight from the guards. "Do you remember what was down there, where you fell?"

"Every item of it, and I want recognition for their unearthing." She glared up at him even as his hand on her arm sent flutters through her stomach. "Don't even think about sneaking them out of the country for your own gain."

He cocked his head, his smile hesitant. "Do you like me, Miss Pencavel?"

"What do you signify?" She was taken aback by this question. "Of course I do. Well, I do now. I like you very much, when I wasn't sure before." She swallowed hard. "All right, I like you far too much for my own good."

"What does that mean, exactly?" He moved against her and she quivered.

"Don't be tiresome, must I spell it out?" Her heartbeat tripled. The dangerous nearness of him made her giddy. "The imperative question is, do you like *me*?"

"Too damned much; far beyond what I should for my own sanity, I have to concede." His eyes smoldered, burning her up. He bent and kissed her mouth.

She gasped, tasting wine on his lips, and the need inside him as he tightened his arms around her. His hand brushed through her hair, and she ran her fingers through his. Her body bubbled with desire. She wanted to melt into him as he pressed her against the hard Roman column.

Lambrick pulled away with a groan, his handsome face flushed. "If we continue, I won't be responsible for what I might do to you—or rather what I would enjoy doing to you."

"Oh, my, that sounds stimulating in the extreme, but you are judicious." She tried to slow her rampant breathing. "What...do you suggest we do about it?"

"All things being considered, I care too much to have an affair, and sully your reputation, such as it is." He heaved a breath. His fingers dug into her shoulders. "I want to do the mad—and will regret this, I'm certain—yet proper thing, and marry you. But you swore you'd never marry at all, and especially not me."

"I believe I might have spoken in haste when I said that." She lowered her gaze, her body in turmoil. She wondered what his chest looked like, naked, and trembled. "I don't wish to become anyone's property; nonetheless, if we could marry, without you owning me, which we can't, I wouldn't be totally adverse to it."

"Could you love me, Miss Pencavel?" His question was gentle, searching.

"Haven't you noticed that I already do?" She met his gaze, her mouth timorous. "Darn you for causing that in me, you rogue."

"And I'm in the untenable, and exasperating, position of loving you as well, you brazen handful." He kissed her again.

Melwyn moaned into the sensual kiss, then laughed when they parted. "We are both in dire trouble then, aren't we?"

He pressed his forehead to hers. "I can't change the English laws, though I could debate them in the House of Lords. However, we could write up an agreement between us, with my solicitor," he scraped his boots along the ground, "that I don't own you or your property."

A green lizard scurried along the broken cobbles and slithered into the weeds.

"Would that hold up in court?" She laughed again, her flesh thrumming. She reached up and touched his mouth. "Never mind. I will be a foolish woman and...marry you, Lord Lambrick, but you'll be in for a precipitous ride."

"Of that I have no doubt. I suppose if I am to be leg-shackled, it should be to you. We are much alike, in our zest for life, and will instill that in our many children. We will have to return to England, to have the banns called, then return here so you may bask in your glory as an archeologist." He grabbed her and kissed her again. "As Lady Lambrick, if you don't mind it too much."

"Perhaps, don't rush me." Her brain clouded after the kiss, and she thought of cool sheets beneath them. "I'm thinking I won't mind the fringe benefits of that position, that is, the intimate ones. Even if I have no knowledge of such things, I reiterate." She'd have to manage this man, and love him, but let him *think* he was in charge, as men liked that. She'd pay the price of ego-stroking—and looked forward to other types of stroking. "What about my artifacts?"

"My men will safeguard them, don't worry." He caressed her shoulders, his fingers playing her like a pianoforte. His thumb then rubbed under her breast. "I'll have them fill in the hole to discourage any onlookers. And I'll bribe the Italian authorities."

Her nipple hardened and she quivered as the heat soared lower. "Off to England then, and matrimonial bliss. I know you'll never bore me." She traced her finger along his manly jaw, inhaling his musky scent. She sighed and shook her head, hoping she wouldn't rue this decision in the morning. "I have much to discuss with you, as we get to know one another better." She smiled into his beaming face. "However, I should be hauled off to Bedlam. Worse than that, my abigail will never let me hear the end of this."

Chapter Seventeen

Aunt Hedra frowned and raised her quizzing glass. "I'm most astounded, Melwyn. I thought you abhorred that gentleman and the very idea of marriage."

"It seems there's a fine line between hate and love, and I fell over it. A happy plunge, as it turns out." Melwyn smiled as she sat in her aunt's opulent parlor in Grosvenor Square. Her agitation, and troubled mind, felt easier. Instead of balking at being tied down, she looked into a future with infinite possibilities, and sensual forays in the bedroom.

"You always were an impulsive gel, and I'll never understand you, it's true." Aunt Hedra settled her curvaceous buttocks into the upholstered wing chair. "Thank goodness we've gotten rid of panniers, as I used to never fit in any chairs. But I digress; do you really love him?"

"Terribly, I'm afraid. I'm to rest here, then return to Cornwall so we may call the banns in his parish church." Melwyn sighed, reliving Griffin's—she thought of him that way now—hot kisses and caresses upon her person. Her flesh tingled. "Papa will be relieved, I daresay. But more importantly, I'm ecstatic."

"You are very young. I hope you're not making a huge mistake." Her aunt smiled indulgently as a maid brought in the tea tray. "Men can be cantankerous creatures, and unduly possessive after marriage."

The maid set the pot, cups, milk jug, and sugar bowl, plus the silver tea things on the Chinese Chippendale style mahogany table with its pierced ledge at top and pierced support for the legs. The elegant piece had pull out candle trays on each side.

"I won't allow him to dominate me. You know I have a resolute mind." Except when he kissed her and more, Melwyn mused to herself. Her body warmed again at the thought. She was becoming a ninny in love, how very alarming.

"Stick to that, my dear. I never gave Penpol the upper hand, and we hummed along fine." Aunt Hedra poured them both tea, chipped lumps off the sugar cone with her sugar nips, and dropped one in each cup. She handed one Wedgewood black basalt dish to her niece. "I suppose I'll have to travel all the way out to Cornwall to attend your nuptials. How inconvenient."

"You used to live there, Auntie; don't you ever miss it?" Melwyn nestled back in the chair, the delicate basalt cup warming her fingers. "The place you spent your misspent youth."

"Gracious no." Her auntie's mouse-skin eyebrows soared. "London is where the action is, opera, theater, shopping; the occasional hanging; who could ask for more."

"Speaking of shopping, I want the newest of gowns for my wedding." Melwyn intended to dazzle Griffin. A dazzled man was always off-balance and more acquiescent. "Let us shop tomorrow in the Strand."

"Turbans are all the kick for the headgear, though may not look right for a wedding. And they'd never fit over my hair." Aunt Hedra primped at her mountain of tresses, where she now had a tiny wooden ship dangling. She was definitely stuck in the styles of decades past—except for eschewing panniers. "I know the perfect modiste to fix you up." Her aunt sipped loudly from her teacup. "We'll go to my seamstress on Bond Street right here in Mayfair."

"That sounds just the thing." Melwyn sipped her tea, the rich flavor pleasing. "I don't know if I've grown up, as my soon-to-be husband wished me to, but I am more sanguine in all this fuss. I just needed to find the right man, and he was betrothed to me from the beginning." She selected a biscuit from the silver plate on the tea tray. "I hope it's only a temporary malady, my compliance, and silliness."

"I dareswear, you are addle-headed. Don't let that deter you from what you insisted you wanted the last time you were here—whatever that was." Aunt Hedra added more milk to her tea, her gaze steady on her niece. "I don't know why I'm encouraging your wild ramblings, when marriage *is* the best thing for you. Nevertheless, you are aware of your intended's shadowy reputation?"

"I am, though have no absolute proof." Melwyn glanced around the parlor with its breakfront mahogany sideboard, striped silk wallpaper, and upholstered settees. She lowered her voice. "I believe he's a privateer. And it makes him all the more attractive to me."

"Hmmm, don't get in over your pretty head, my dear. Make certain he desists from that nonsense before you wed." Her aunt sighed. "Oh, before I forget. I've had a few notes from that young man you met at Almack's. He kept asking if you were in town." She tapped her chin. "Mr. Showreynolds, the baron's son."

"He probably wanted to know if it was safe for him to go out in public after Gri...Lord Lambrick threatened him." Melwyn laughed, remembering the stumbling dullard in question. She did feel somewhat sorry for the young man. "My fiancé is so forceful and masculine, he can't help himself."

"Bother it all, I've forgotten something else. I have a meeting of the Ladies Garden Society out in Kew tomorrow. I'm lecturing on rose hybrids, and I am the reigning expert." Aunt Hedra set down her cup with a click in its saucer. "But I'll give you a letter of introduction to Madame Vêtements, my modiste. You can take your common gel with you as escort."

****

The following day, Melwyn was measured in the back of a shop by an officious Frenchwoman of at least forty years of age. "Oh, *Mademoiselle*, you have the loveliest figure, yes? I will make you the divine gown. A round gown of white clear muslin; chemise sleeves, festooned with lace, and tied with a riband of burgundy color. The dress will be braided in the back, and bound round the neck with a second broad burgundy riband, and a plaiting of lace." The petite Madame Vêtements waved the measuring tape in the air, her tight black curls bouncing. "You must purchase some white silk shoes for the occasion."

"She be lookin' like an angel, though an imp in cherub's clothing," Clowenna said with a roll of her eyes. "Set to marry that devil o' a man *I* said she loved, an' *she* denied it over an' over. But that be a match made in Heaven, or Hell, them two."

"The dress sounds *très parfait*, Madame. Let's hope for Heaven, shall we?" Melwyn stepped off the stool, her chemise whispering around her, and cast her abigail a sharp stare. "Sew something fancy for Mrs. Buckett as well, with several fuchsia ribands, yards of pink lace, massive furbelows and other frippery."

"I hate lace an' don't care much for ruffles." Clowenna plucked several ribbons from the samples laid out, all browns and muted yellows. "An' in pink I'll look like a stuffed pig."

"Breadcrumbs will become you; and I'd love to stick an apple in your mouth on occasion, out of affection of course." Melwyn wrapped her stays around her, and her maid laced them up. Then she slipped her gown over her chemise. She ran her fingers along the sleek silk and satin cloth, and plush, rich velvets of the material on display. "I suppose I'll have to order many gowns to show well as Lady Lambrick."

"Still, the valet might like me in lace." Clowenna picked up a strip of Venetian lace and swept it around her throat. "Kenver be a man o' good taste."

"Do I detect a romance blooming?" Melwyn laughed when her abigail blushed. But she wasn't certain how she felt about Clowenna seeking interests elsewhere. Melwyn's heart sank a notch. Selfishly, she'd planned for the maid, her friend, to remain in her employ forever. "At the ripe old age of seven and twenty, you've found a beau? Impossible."

"No one is ever too old for love, *mes belles dames*. You English are so stiff upper lip." Madame Vêtements scribbled down the measurements. "I will have this for you in three days, if we work very hard, *non*."

"I will come in for a fitting before I leave for Padstow. If the gown needs alterations, you may finish them then send it to me there." Melwyn thanked the woman and left the shop. Out on Bond Street, carriages and people bustled by, the scents of perfume, sea coal smoke and horses mixing together. "I never thought I'd be planning a wedding, instead of an expedition. Papa must have fainted dead away when he received my letter."

"I'm certain once the bloom wears off, 'ee be off again to scrabble in the dirt an' fall in holes." Clowenna wrinkled her nose. She stepped around a pile of dog poop after a grand lady's poodle crouched and did his duty. "This city still stinks."

"I would like to visit Egypt after Italy, and investigate the pyramids. But I hope my husband will go with me." Sultry nights in the desert beside her beloved, with the braying of a camel in the background, how perfect! She'd be famous by then after her discovery in Pompeii. She dearly hoped the artifacts remained protected and hidden. "Hail us a hackney and we'll look for a shoemaker's shop. I need those silk slippers to look fashionably stunning."

"Oh, la, 'ee be like someone I never met afore." Clowenna widened her eyes in theatrical shock. "But

I'm that glad you're marryin' him. Rein 'ee both in, it will."

At that moment a fine coach pulled up to the sidewalk. A familiar face leaned out the window. "By jingo, Lady Pencavel. How good to see you again." The bland features of Mr. Showreynolds smiled from under a beige bicorn hat. "May I offer you a ride to wherever you need to go?"

Melwyn hesitated, fighting down a wince. The young man, who she must have scandalized horribly at Almack's, acted overly friendly now. Why had he written her aunt to inquire after her? "You need not trouble yourself, Mr. Showreynolds. I will hire a hackney. We're only shopping. But thank you for offering."

"It's no trouble. Please, allow me to smooth over the misconceptions and blunders of our previous meeting." He opened the coach door, his gaze earnest. "My coach is quite comfortable. Much finer than a hackney. And these London jarvey's are not to be trusted."

Melwyn was in a joyous mood and hated to be rude—a peculiar situation for her. "Very well. Perhaps you know a respected shoemaker close by. I require a pair of silk slippers." She didn't know if he was aware of her pending nuptials and decided not to mention it. "You are too kind in stopping."

"I am honored to do so, I assure you. There's a fine slipper shop over on Oxford Street. My mother praises the work they do there." Showreynolds let down the step, his grin wide.

"The honor is mine, sir." Melwyn's guilt at her previous actions seeped through her. She'd have to apologize. She picked up her skirt and petticoat hem and stepped up. He reached out and assisted her inside the plush interior that smelled much fresher than any hackney. She settled on the seat across from him.

Clowenna climbed up on the step to enter. Showreynolds rose again, pushed her back and slammed the coach door shut. The maid stumbled down to the sidewalk.

"What do you think you're *doing*? You might have hurt her." Melwyn's heart jumped, her mind numb with shock. She reached for the door handle as the coach clattered off over the paving stones. "Halt this vehicle this instant. I'm leaving, you despicable boor!"

Showreynolds held up a tiny pistol and waved it in her face. His eyes darted nervously. "Not so fast, Miss Pencavel. You will be coming with me, and paying for your-your humiliating actions."

****

Griffin faced the disturbed face of his neighbor, Mr. Trefoile, in Merther Manor's front hall. "I apologize for any misinterpretation. I repeat, there was no understanding between me and your daughter, sir." He resisted saying "milksop of a daughter" as that would have been a tad insulting, and he'd risen above such things.

"I beg to differ, sir. My girl is heartbroken that you called the banns this morning in church for a union with another." Trefoile hooked his thumbs in the lapels of his claret-colored frock coat. His protruding belly resembled a giant tomato. "I nearly stood up to protest."

"Give her my deepest regrets." Griffin recalled the sharp weeping coming from a few pews back. The poor, deluded girl. He hoped Miss Pencavel would arrive soon, and intimidate everyone into submission. "However, I was betrothed to Earl Pencavel's daughter first."

He longed to be alone with her, kissing her vigorously, and more, soon, much more. He needed her, and her soft charms; her tart tongue was always a challenge—nevertheless, he was up to conquering her. His blood sizzled, but he shook off the sensual haze.

Trefoile eyed him balefully. "Regrets won't do, sir, no not at all. I'm extremely perturbed."

"Then how can I recompense you? A ewe or two?" Griffin was anxious to get rid of his unwanted visitor. Before leaving for Italy, he'd sold his stash of artifacts. But another ship was due this evening. The thrill of the illegal maneuver should have coursed through him by now. He pondered its absence, warm with relief that he'd decided to make this his last attempt.

"Don't suppose I'm not aware of your, shall I say, illicit doings here," Trefoile said as if reading Griffin's mind. His neighbor dragged his fingers through greasy, pomaded hair, which stunk of beef fat. "I'm not to be hoodwinked, as you did to my girl."

"I don't know what you allude to, in either case. I'm very busy, so if you will please excuse me," Griffin fought a cringe and opened his front door, "I bid you good day, sir. I'll send over the sheep." He'd been about to offer the man a Roman trinket, but now that was out of the question.

"Sheep in exchange for my daughter's downtrodden heart? I think you do know of what I allude to, Lambrick. Most of us in the area know, but never speak of, the unseemly monkey business down in your cove." Trefoile wagged a plump finger. "That could change at any moment."

"I dearly hope you aren't threatening me, Trefoile." Griffin kept his voice smooth, even as his hackles rose. He hovered over the much shorter man. "I am Viscount of Merther, and the premier peer in the region. I would be Justice of the Peace, except for that derelict duke who resides on the other side of the vale." Griffin had profited because the duke *was* so languid in his duties.

"I just advise you, that's all. You should never toy with a sensitive girl's feelings. She so wanted to be a viscountess." Trefoile slapped on his hat, waddled out the door and down the steps, to his waiting curricle.

Griffin closed the door with a sigh. He *must* make tonight's endeavor his last; he'd been assured it was a special and profitable shipment. He thought of the exquisite treasure still being guarded by his men in Pompeii. But he'd have to leave that trove for Miss Pencavel's glorification. He smiled. She'd be quite grateful for that.

"Is your visitor, the oh so proper Mr. Trefoile, not staying for tea? The poor, disappointed man, with such a dear, sweet daughter." Mrs. Loveday drifted in, her eyes red as she sniffed into her handkerchief. "There are crumpets, too."

"Oh, please stop your blubbering. And bursting into tears in church along with Miss Trefoile was quite discomfiting." Griffin pressed his housekeeper's shoulder, the familiar steadiness in his life. "You should be happy that I'm settling down and we'll soon hear the pitter patter of tiny feet about the place."

"But Miss Pencavel, of all women. I pray you don't lament the day, sir." She blew her nose loudly. "The girl may behave so distastefully, you'll never beget an heir. If she's like her mother, you won't know whose child it is."

"I doubt that very much. We love each other, as befuddled as that sounds. Give her a chance, for my sake." Griffin winked over any qualms. "Between you and I, we'll train her to be the ideal Lady Lambrick." He chuckled, aiming to placate, praying that was true. "I will rely on you, as always."

"She may be beyond even my prodigious talents." Mrs. Loveday squeezed his elbow. "I fear for you, sir. But I will do my best." She stuffed her handkerchief in her apron pocket then fingered the chatelaine always worn around her waist. This decorative clasp held a series of chains, each attached to a useful item: scissors, a thimble, and her precious keys. "I will be certain to keep the servants' hall locked."

Mrs. Loveday squared her shoulders and left him.

He rubbed the back of his neck; so many disturbances. *Did* he know Miss Pencavel well enough to trust her around his staff? He swiped that from his brain. She adored him, he saw it in her eyes during the entire voyage back to England, even as her maid barfed over the rail.

Yet they were still like two lions circling one another.

Griffin went to his library and pored over his accounts until the sun dipped low. The maids came through and lit candles, sending the sweet scent of beeswax into the air.

"Sorry, I'm late, sir. Me old woman had the megrims an' me supper were delayed. More truthfully, when I asked for supper, she bounced a pot off me head." Jacca entered and removed his round hat. He rubbed a bump on his scalp. His glum face appeared hound dog weary in the flickering candlelight. "I trust the accounts are in order."

"I have much to look forward to in wedded bliss I see. I don't know how you've put up with such violence all these years." Griffin forced a laugh, tapping his quill on the books. Could he manage his own wildcat? "Everything looks in order."

"I'm too much the cully with the missus. Ess, good about the accounts. Ready to go to the cove, sir?" Jacca shoved a pistol in his waistband and replaced his hat.

Griffin slipped on his frock coat and the two fetched lanterns, a few other men, and walked stealthily down to the cove.

The cool, early October air caressed his face. A cormorant called in the reeds. The sun's last rays slipped over the horizon. Trefoile's warning churned like a spiked wheel in Griffin's thoughts.

He breathed deeply. After this, he would embrace the life of a married man, and oh, what a vixen he'd have in his bed. Hopefully soon he'd be a doting father.

The light receded, the twilight descending slowly, like a black veil dropped lightly over the landscape. The saline scent of the ocean filled his nostrils.

They waited, the wind rustling the grass. Waves slurped the shingle below. Griffin shifted in his jackboots, anxious for the sight of a sail.

Soon he was rewarded. A sail was spotted; the sea calm, the ship seemed to float toward them, not tossed or harried. His heartbeat increased, the hunt, the terrible risk.

The ship signaled. Griffin raised his lantern and signaled in return.

"What would you say if I told you that this will absolutely be my last incursion into smuggling?"

"You've mentioned such. But I'd not believe 'ee, pardon me sayin', sir." Jacca fumbled with this flint and steel, lighting his clay pipe. "Then what will *I* do to amuse meself?"

"Find a mistress, and separate from your wife," Griffin blurted. "But I'm set on it. I want to settle down and have a family. I will inform all my contacts to look elsewhere for a privateer." He chuckled, then stiffened at the sound of footsteps on the slope above them. Pebbles skittered down like grapeshot. He glared up but saw nothing.

"The jig may be up," Jacca whispered.

A nightjar trebled in the bushes, disturbed. A glowworm glimmered like an eerie green alarm. The hairs on the back of Griffin's neck bristled.

"Halt what you're doing!" a voice shouted. "We're the king's men. Or rather, *halt in the name of the king*!"

"Blast and damn," Griffin muttered, his muscles clenching.

Two men scrambled down through the brush. One stood beside Griffin, musket raised.

"Grif, I'm sorry to catch you here. I really am," the sheriff said when he strode into their lantern light. "I'm also deeply disappointed in you."

"We're partaking of the night air. Nothing wrong with that, Raw, my old friend," Griffin replied through tight lips, his stomach sinking. How had he been so careless tonight? "This is my private property, and quite picturesque in the autumn season."

Jacca stared straight ahead, puffing on his pipe. Smoke snaked about them both.

"I saw you signal that ship. This is not a designated port of call. I warned you, Grif." Rawlyn sighed morosely, shaking his head. "I'm afraid there's no help for it, I'll have to arrest you."

Chapter Eighteen

"You are insane, and infinitely imprudent, if I may be so frank." Melwyn paced the chamber of the townhouse, which was situated God knew where. She suspected London, as she heard the clang and bell chimes of the city out the window. "You cannot hold me here indefinitely."

The stained wallpaper and sour smell disquieted her further.

"I'll hold you until you do my bidding." Showreynolds sat in a Windsor chair, the pistol butt balanced on his knee. His sandy hair was mussed and his bland face in a grimace. The stink of sweat emanated from him.

"And I've told you that is out of the question." She used bravado to glaze over her uneasiness. She couldn't allow this nothing of a young man to intimidate her, though she really disliked the gun aspect. Her body trembled a bit. "Please let me go and we can forget this ever happened."

"N-Not until I get what I want." He waved the pistol, his hazel eyes wide.

"I will *not* give you my virtue. I'm saving it for my future husband." She swallowed slowly, thinking of Griffin's dark eyes and deep voice, so different from this non-entity. Would she ever see her beloved again? She stifled a groan. "Now please respect my sensibilities."

"After the brazen way you behaved at Almack's, I'm not certain you possess any such attributes." He crossed and uncrossed his legs in their white stockings. His beige breeches hugged his stocky thighs tightly.

"I can't fault you there, Mr. Showreynolds. I behaved abominably, and I again apologize." She dipped her head and walked toward the window, away from the narrow bed in the corner. "It's stuffy in here, don't you think? May I open this casement for fresh air?"

"Of course, as you will." He nodded, then sputtered and glared at her. "No, step away from the window. You can't fool me; you want to call for help."

"You're so very astute, sir." She crossed her arms and paced back the way she'd come. She must find a way out of here.

"And don't you forget my cleverness. I even followed you in the British Museum where you pretended to study artifacts."

"I *do* study artifacts. So that was you cowering behind the statue of Zeus?" She regretted that statement the moment it left her lips.

"I'm no coward!" He pointed the tiny pistol, his hand unsteady. "And I'm not the-the coxcomb you m-might think I am either."

"I never thought of you in any such fashion." Mouth dry, she raised her chin, pretending the idea of a bullet piercing her flesh mattered little. "Does your father approve of your actions?"

"He does not know. The Baron always supposes I'm a wimp of the first order." His mouth gaped. "How dare you impinge on my father's good character."

"When the *ton* finds out what you've done, won't that put a teeny blot on his character?" She gripped her elbows. Her breath hitched as genuine fear pricked her. "Or do you plan to kill me and hide my body somewhere?"

"Kill? No one said anything about m-murder." He scratched his cheek with the pistol barrel. "I may not have planned this out to the best of my ability."

"Then let me assist you, if I may." Hope rose up, relaxing her a fraction. "Nothing has happened yet—other than a kidnapping and you manhandling my servant—so let us return outside. You call me a hackney, and pay for it as you've inconvenienced me, and—"

"Silence, you immodest coquette!" Showreynolds stood, scraping back the chair. "Don't think you can talk your way out of this situation. Or-or that your Lord Lambrick will come to your aid this time. And I found out he's not a member of your family."

"Oh, that, only a harmless prevarication on my part." She shrugged and tried a regretful smile. She did need to think about the feelings of others more thoroughly. "I am truly sorry I ruffled your feathers, sir. Can't you forgive me my trespasses, as the Bible intones?"

"Don't pull religion on me, Miss Pencavel." He stretched to his not-so-impressive middling height. "My family is a respected High Church family from the time of Elizabeth I. We held strong during the turbulence of Cromwell as well."

"My family is High Church, when we do go." She narrowed her eyes at him. Her father had given up on religion when her debauched mother deserted him. "I had no idea that kidnapping innocent women was a High Church tenet."

"There is your ill-conceived tongue again." He stalked toward her, pistol raised.

"I agree, it has always gotten me into trouble." She thrust out her hand to hold him back, her heart twitching. "I can arrange for monetary compensation for your unfortunate insult at my selfish actions. I'm sure my betrothed-again, Lord Lambrick, will pay handsomely for my release."

"You're *betrothed* to that rapscallion?" Showreynold's mouth nearly gaped to the floor. His voice rose to a high-pitch. "Will the affronts never end?"

"I meant to keep that to myself, so forget I spoke." Melwyn cursed inwardly. Perspiration gathered under her arms as she watched his crazed expression. "But if money is what you—"

"Enough!" He poked the pistol into her chin. "I'm getting what I abducted you for, you heartless hussy—but p-please don't be upset afterwards."

Melwyn squirmed. She grabbed for the barrel while ducking her head to avoid having it shot off. "Unhand me, you spineless sprig! I'm beyond furious now!"

Showreynolds growled and pushed her down on the bed. His fingers groped at her neckline, and she screamed and kicked at him. The pistol clattered to the floor.

****

Griffin stood in the anteroom of the Bodmin Jail, a place he had no intention of spending any more time than necessary in. He took a steadying breath to calm himself. "Raw, really, what did you actually see. Me blinking my lantern? What mischief is there in that? I was guiding the ship around our treacherous shoals, that's all."

"I wish I could leave it at that, Grif." Rawlyn leaned against his desk, his bony shoulders hunched. "But I had a complaint from a prosperous citizen. I can't ignore such accusations."

"I know the citizen in question, and he has a bone to pick with me over his aspirations that I would wed his daughter." Griffin's jaw tightened as he thought of Trefoile. "The man has a vendetta against me."

"Why wouldn't you wed his daughter? The entire region laments that it's far beyond time you took a wife." Rawlyn looked genuinely puzzled. "Miss Trefoile isn't that off-putting to look at, and her dowry is generous."

"I'm in love with another, if you must pry." Griffin strode across the room, lovely blue eyes softening his anger. "Which reminds me. I need to get word to my fiancée, who is probably traveling from London to Cornwall. I don't want her to worry."

"Is it that fetching lady I met that day at Merther Manor? I'll let you have paper and ink." Rawlyn plucked up a quill from his desk. "But I'll have to hold you over for the quarterly assizes, Grif. I have no choice."

"I refuse to spend another night in that pit in your cellar." Griffin brushed down his sleeves for emphasis. He'd heard rats in the walls all night long. He fought a grimace. "I am a man of refined tastes, after all."

"Our gaol is fairly new. The buildings were designed by Sir John Call, Bart. J.P., M.P. in 1778, and based on the plans and ideals of the prison reformer John Howard," Rawlyn intoned, his brow creased in annoyance. "Bodmin Gaol is a milestone in prison design."

"Yes, yes, I've heard it all. It's light and airy and therefore healthy, with different isolated areas for felons, misdemeanants and debtors." Griffin strutted about the room, throwing a hand in the air. His father had contributed to its erection. Griffin thanked God his father couldn't see his downfall. "There is hot water, a chapel, an infirmary for sick prisoners and individual sleeping cells. Very good, but I don't wish to inhabit the place for long."

"Plus, don't forget, your valet was in attendance, at my permission." Rawlyn smirked as he pulled paper from a desk drawer. "I understand you supped on roast mutton and good claret, hardly the feast of the subjugated."

"Kenver? He's mooning over my betrothed's abigail, so not quite so attentive a valet as I'd like. He brought me the second-best claret, and the mutton was slightly gristly." Griffin sighed and shook his head at the vagaries of servants. "Kenver and the sham Mrs. Bucket seem to have formed an attachment." And Griffin understood well how a man could be distracted by a woman.

"I'll put you in a better cell, closer to the necessary, if that will help." Rawlyn held up a ring of jangling keys, his gaze almost sympathetic. "I did warn you to cease your nocturnal high jinks."

"You can't be serious. I'm a peer, and should be above such things." For the first time, the idea he could spend years in prison crept through Griffin, dampening his core. How would he enjoy intimate moments with Miss Pencavel, or sire children, if he was locked away? What would happen to Merther Manor without him there to guide her? He'd also miss his horse!

"Sir! Sir!" A familiar voice called. Jacca appeared, red in the face, a constable gripping his arm and dragged along behind. "I have a confession to make."

"What is the meaning of this commotion?" Rawlyn thrust his hands on his nonexistent hips.

"I took him for his walk, as prisoners get a short walk, but he insisted on coming in here," the constable stammered. "He's strong for an old bugger."

"Sirs, Sheriff Tremayne an' Lord Lambrick. I must be allowed to confess." Jacca staggered over to them, the constable still hanging on his arm.

"Confess to what?" Griffin asked as he opened a bottom drawer in the sheriff's desk where he knew brandy was stashed. Jacca wasn't about to spill the beans, give them up, and thus ruin everything? His anger heated up. "Surely you have naught to say. As your employer, I do object."

"That's *my* question as an officer of the law, if you don't mind," Rawlyn grumbled. He turned to Jacca. "Confess to what, bailiff?"

"I did it all, alone, the smugglin', the sellin' of artifacts from them foreign ports. An' never once did I pay no taxes. I were a miscreant." Jacca raised his arm high. "The king should want to shoot me personal."

"No, don't lie for me," Griffin protested, stunned by this turn of events. "I refuse to allow it. Though I appreciate the sentiment, you're carrying allegiance far too far."

"'Tisn'no lie. It were all me doin' an' his lordship knew nothin'."

"Don't be foolhardy, bailiff. We caught your master with you," Rawlyn said, bemusement in this tone. "As much as I'd like to set him free, I simply can't."

"He were tryin' to stop me, he was." Jacca bowed toward Griffin. "Lord Lambrick be an upstanding citizen of the realm. No better man anywhere, I'll be bound."

"Jacca, please, this isn't necessary," Griffin said, infused with shame. He uncorked the brandy and took a gulp of the smoky liquid "I insist that you desist and—"

"But it is! 'Ee think I want to go home to me old woman? Nearly lost me scalp last time the harridan went at me." Jacca heaved a troubled breath. "I hope they'll convict me an' transport me to the Americas.

Oh, wait, we lost them didn't we? Then that land down under, Aussietrailia. That'll be far enough away from the brutal witch."

"Jacca, you don't know what you're saying." Griffin clasped his bailiff's shoulder, choked up by the man's loyalty, and his desperation to flee his spouse. "Rawlyn, you can't consider what he's admitting to as the sole perpetrator? However, I won't admit that any crime took place so there was nothing to perpetrate."

"Believe it, Sheriff. I'm the one 'ee want." Jacca nodded his glum face vigorously, and the man did look the happiest ever. "Just me an' no one else."

"How could you have pulled this off from right under your master's nose?" Rawlyn stared in skepticism from Griffin to Jacca. "As much as I'd like to believe you."

"I'm a sneaky old codger, an' the master be a heavy sleeper." The bailiff poked the sheriff and winked. "I'll show 'ee the secret tunnel under the estate. I dug it meself."

"I beg you to think this over." Griffin wrestled with the scruples he was surprised to possess. His face seared. "How can I allow you to take the blame?" He glanced at Rawlyn. "If there *was* any crime to be admitted to in the first instance, which there is not."

"But I *need* to do it, being I'm the guilty one, sir, an' 'ee were totally ignorant." Jacca's eyes pleaded with him, his hands gripped together in supplication. "I'd be quite the jackaroo down under, I would."

"I can picture you herding kangaroos," Griffin said dryly, realizing how truly desperate his bailiff was to escape the country. His stomach started to unknot.

He would have his glorious wedding. He turned to the sheriff. "Raw, can I get a guarantee my man will be transported and not simply incarcerated or hung?"

"I'd take the rope over seein' me old woman again," Jacca admitted.

"I suppose arrangements can be made, greasing the right palms as is the custom." Rawlyn sighed, snatched the brandy bottle from Griffin and took his own gulp. "You're released, Grif. And I sincerely hope you've learned your lesson."

"I believe I have. I am in your debt, both of you." Griffin began to relax; no more smuggling for him. Miss Pencavel, or rather soon to be Mrs. Lambrick, would be all the stimulation he required. He grasped Jacca's hand. "Take care of yourself, my good man. Stay clear of the wallabies."

"Your lordship, if I may be so rude as to interrupt." Kenver rushed over, the valet immaculate in his striped waistcoat and perfectly knotted cravat. He removed his hat and pressed it to his broad chest.

Griffin felt disheveled in comparison, after a night in a dingy cell. He scratched at an itch in his side. "You may. Then you may follow me home and draw me a hot bath. I pray I won't need a delousing."

"I have an urgent note from Lady Pencavel's aunt, Lady Penpol." Kenver handed him the note.

Griffin broke the seal. His heart clenched as he read. "Deuce it all. My beloved has been abducted by a crazed baron's son. I must away to London to save her." As only he could, being the brave—and now honest—hero that he wished to embody.

Chapter Nineteen

Melwyn wriggled violently under the heaving form of Mr. Showreynolds. His knees bumped her legs, his fingers ripping at her bodice. His stocky body squeezed the air from her chest. She writhed about, then bit his ear, tasting flesh and blood.

"Ouch, you bitch!" he cried as he jerked back. "Give me leave to unbutton my breeches."

"Fie! You dare to chastise me, when you're the one abusing my person?" She strained to catch her breath. With all her strength she shoved him to the floor. Scrambling to her feet, she picked up a chamber pot and smashed it over his head. "You couldn't take a simple apology? You were badly raised, sir."

"You are a heartless wench," he groaned as glass shards scattered over the room. He slumped to the planks, blood trickling down his face.

She snatched up the pistol and ran to the door. "I'll tell your father and the authorities where to find you. If I feel so inclined." She hurried down the stairs and out the front door. Her pulse skittering, she brushed back her hair with shaking fingers.

She felt for the coins in her inside pocket, thankful they were still there. She finally hailed a hackney, as most of the jarvies stared at her rumpled visage in suspicion, and she returned to her aunt's in Grosvenor Square.

"Oh, my poor darling. How I worried!" Aunt Hedra embraced her in a puff of lavender and pomade. "I'll send a missive to a Bow Street Runner to apprehend that churlish knave."

"I hope they parade him through the streets naked." Melwyn sighed in relief to be free, then frowned, chewing her lower lip. "On second thought, no one wants to witness that ugly spectacle."

"Oh, la, you're not dead an' dropped into a ditch in the city." Clowenna hugged her fiercely. "Let's leave this den of iniquity called London."

"No, not yet. The poor gel must rest after this frightening incident." Aunt Hedra scrutinized Melwyn through her quizzing glass. "Be that as it may, you are still virginal, aren't you, Mellie?"

"Indeed I am, Auntie. Only a little bruised, but not where it might count." Melwyn stared up at her aunt's hair, where now a string of pearls was entwined like a path of snow winding up a peak. "At least I finished my gown measurements before I was kidnapped. The dress will be exquisite."

"I'll prepare a bath, as 'ee greatly need one." Clowenna waved her hand before her face. "But I'm that glad 'ee wasn't raped an' left to fend for yourself in a St. Giles rookery."

"I can't rest too long. I must journey to Padstow, and the dashing Lord Lambrick. I've missed him so." She never thought she'd say that, Melwyn mused with a silly laugh as her chest heaved then heated with desire. "I need his strong arms to hold me. And I have a wedding, my own, to attend."

"'Ee might be more a trial, that is too smarmy, in love, I do fear," Clowenna groused as she helped her mistress up the Adam's staircase.

"I'll order the servants to haul up buckets of hot water at once." Aunt Hedra bustled toward her kitchen, petticoats rustling and pearls clicking. "Then send for that Bow Street Runner. Hopefully one with more astuteness than the one searching for you."

"You weren't hurt, were you, Clowie, when that dastardly baron's brat pushed you?" Melwyn fought a shudder, reliving her and her abigail's ordeal. They entered the guest bedchamber.

"Naw. Only bruised me bum a bit." Clowenna helped her mistress out of her torn and dirty clothes. "Your aunt sent word to his lordship 'bout what happened."

"That will take days to reach him, then he'll take days—because I'm certain he'll want to rush here—to reach me." Melwyn checked the scratches on her body, wincing at the soreness. "I must write immediately to let him know I'm all right, but then that letter will no doubt miss him in transit."

Several maids hurried in with steaming buckets of water, which they poured into a copper bathtub. Melwyn donned a clean chemise and lowered herself into the soothing water. She scrubbed her skin with Crown soap while Clowenna washed her hair in dissolved soap shavings, then rinsed her tresses with lemon juice, to remove the sticky soap.

Melwyn luxuriated in the attention. Dried off, she sat before the vanity and her maid brushed her hair to bring back the natural oils.

"I suppose you're anxious to see the valet?" Melwyn smiled at her in the mirror.

"I might be. Then again, maybe not." Clowenna's face turned a slight shade of pink.

"Don't be shy, admit your attachment." Melwyn laughed, then groaned. "I am a silly ninny goose, seeing love everywhere. I wonder when the intoxication will wear off."

"Soon, like I said afore, m'lady. We can only hope." The maid raked the bristles through Melwyn's hair. "Or did that absconder thrash 'ee in the head?"

Melwyn preened at the ripples on her scalp. "No, my precious if abrasive abigail, but I did bite his ear. Nasty taste." She checked her teeth as she stared at her tired reflection. "Prepare me a sage and salt rub for my mouth. I'll rest for two days, go to my fitting at the modiste, then hire a post-chaise to Cornwall. We should catch his lordship on the London Road."

****

Griffin spurred the hired horse down the London Road. At each night's stop, he'd hired a fresh horse while trying not to acquire lice or fleas from the inns. When possible, he cut through meadows and heaths. His thighs and back ached from the constant riding at a gallop, but he needed to save Miss Pencavel. He'd strangle that blunder-headed Mr. Showreynolds if he'd ravished his bride to be. No one would dare touch her, except for Griffin.

However, if he was too late, and she was no longer pure, but damaged goods, what could he do? A woman's maidenhead was everything, as every man wanted to be the first, to go where no man had gone before. If he lived by the creed of the time, he'd have to think twice about accepting a ruined woman.

He groaned, and kicked the horse into a faster gallop. No, he wouldn't care; he loved her and no one else. And after all, he was hardly perfect either.

To adore someone so completely completed him. Who was to know this sprite of a girl, even with her quarrelsome mouth, would be his perfect match? He could almost forget the tragic loss of his brother in her arms.

Pebbles flying around him, the scent of trees earthy and sharp, mingled with the sweat of horseflesh, he spotted a post-chaise in the distance. Griffin slowed his mount so as not to frighten the oncoming team.

The small coach drew closer in a jangle of harnesses. A curtain twitched aside, and a young woman opened the window and stuck out her head. "Griffin, is that you? What good fortune and coincidence."

"Halt," he ordered the driver of the coach. "I need to speak to your passengers."

The man pulled in his team, then jerked out a blunderbuss. "If you plan to rob me, sir, I'll blow your head off. I've got the Royal mail and two innocent women on board."

"Have a care, my diligent friend! I'm Lord Lambrick, the Viscount of Mercer, not a highwayman." Griffin held up his hand. "I believe you have my betrothed with you."

Griffin stopped his horse, who snorted and coughed, foam on its lips. He dismounted and approached. The coach door swung open, and the lovely Miss Pencavel stepped out.

"I thought you were kidnapped." He threw up his hands, chagrined and relieved at the same time. "I'm on my way to rescue you."

"I freed myself, dear Griffin. I slammed a chamber pot over the lout's head." She laughed and his heart puddled.

"You've quite taken the wind out of my sails." He stepped close, into her fragrant smell of lemon, and touched a tendril of her honey-blonde hair that had fallen from its coiffure. "Who am I to defend now? My swashbuckling is terribly put out." He pulled her against him, so soft and pliant, and kissed her sweet lips.

"You may defend me for the rest of your life." She trailed her fingers down his chest.

"Did the cretin hurt you, sully you in any way?" he had to ask. "Not that it matters to me in the least."

"No, I prevented any sullying. I'm saving myself for you, sir." She leaned close and whispered, "you may have me fresh for all your depraved pleasures."

"Ah, and depraved they will be. Two more Sundays to call the banns." Griffin caressed her shoulders as his body inflamed like sizzling coal. "In fact, since I'd miss this Sunday, riding on a futile rescue as it turns out, I asked my housekeeper to make certain they're called." He recalled Mrs. Loveday's burst into tears when he'd made his request. "I had to pay her double for the trouble."

"I cannot wait to be your wife. I said some pretty nasty things to you earlier in our odd courtship. I hope you'll forgive me." She stood on tiptoe and kissed him.

"I thought you a brainless hoyden, but was soon disavowed of that notion. I'm heartily glad you are a saucy woman of substance." He captured her lips again, reveling in her taste. His body reacted, a slow tantalizing tingle. "I can't wait for our wedding night."

"Then we go to Italy for our honeymoon." Miss Pencavel sighed in obvious contentment. "And to display my grand find and savor my success."

"I don't know who my once spirited lady has become." The maid now poked her head out. "You've quite flummoxed her, sir. 'Tis a miracle, but peculiar just the same."

"I'm only softening him for the kill." Miss Pencavel laughed and stroked Griffin's cheek.

"Enough of this twaddle, I have a schedule to meet," the driver grumbled. He still held the blunderbuss in his lap, his trigger finger twitching. "I've vital mail to deliver."

"I'll ride beside the coach on our way to Merther Manor, my love. We don't wish to be shot before we begin our lives together." Griffin assisted Miss Pencavel back into the coach and returned to his overridden horse. The animal tried to nip his leg in protest.

Chapter Twenty

Melwyn studied the small painting on the wall behind Griffin's desk. A handsome young man in a red army officer's uniform, with gold braid around the high collar. "This is your brother Alan?"

"Yes. He was killed four years ago, in 1792, at the Battle of Jemappes in the Austrian Netherlands, now called Belgium after being annexed by France." Griffin frowned sadly. "I just put the painting back up. I couldn't look at it for a long time."

She took his hand and squeezed it. "I'm so sorry for your loss. I can't imagine the hurt, since I never had siblings, though mother seemed busy enough in that department."

"They broke the mold after you were cast, my love." He embraced her; the warmth from his muscled chest sent shivers into her own tender breasts. "I became an even worse devil after his death, to prove myself I suppose. I dared the excise men to shoot me, and they finally did."

She winced at that statement and stroked his shoulder. "I'm deeply grateful you weren't killed. Alan must have been very dear to you."

"We were close, only two years apart. Since I'd inherit the title, Alan wanted to make a name for himself in the army." He glanced away. "I blamed myself after he died."

"As I blamed myself for my mother's desertion." She cringed, recalling her ugly encounter with that less-than-admirable person. "Now I see how wrong I was. I hope you see that as well.

"Emotions aren't so easily tied up into neat little bows." He smiled ironically. His fingers on her flesh almost fogged her brain.

"I agree. If we want to wail and whine about our lives once in a while, we'll do it together." Melwyn puzzled for a moment. "But we weren't yet at war with France in 1792. Why was your brother there?"

"No, we weren't in conflict as yet." Now Griffin wrinkled his brow in contemplation. "I'm afraid Alan jumped the gun a bit, anticipating that we would soon be in combat. France declared war on us but a few months later."

"I demure at saying this, but are you certain he wasn't up to some illegal maneuvering with foreign troops?"

"Ah, my perfect brother may have had a fault? That does give me pause." The lines around Griffin's eyes relaxed. "I still insist he died valiantly in battle."

"And we're still deep in war. The French have repelled Austria from Italy and created their own republics there." She glanced around this masculine room, in dire need of a woman's touch, though she wasn't the doily-draping, sample-stitching sort of girl.

"What about your mother?" He watched her, his mahogany eyes delving deep inside her as no one else ever had...or dared. "Have you no pity for her at all?"

"I've wavered over this intensely. I suppose I should pity someone who has no impulse control, and a lack of moral compass. I used to worry that was me, but I just hadn't found my debonair knight." She scrutinized her intended. His broad, muscular shoulders and slender hips. She sighed with yearning. "I still think you'd look incredibly urbane in a gladiator's toga."

"I might don one for you on our wedding night." He gave his cocky smile, the one that melted her heart. "Or I'll sneak over to the guest cottage tonight and inveigle a tournament."

She laughed, half wishing he would. "Remember my father is due here today." She was staying at his guest cottage a quarter mile from the main house, until the wedding.

"Well, at last the final banns have been called as I am an impatient groom." He winked suggestively.

"Who was that woman in the black veil weeping in church this morning?" Melwyn had felt a malevolent stare from that direction. "And the dull-eyed girl who tossed her prayer book at me? Thank goodness she has terrible aim."

Griffin chuckled. "Not everyone is enthusiastic about our union." He crushed her against his pelvis and his form-fitting nankeen breeches that enveloped him like a second skin. "But I'm the only one who you have to please."

"Soon, my love. I can tell you anticipate our joining." She moved away a step, her face flushing. A heat started low in her belly. "As I have no knowledge of such things, even if we women should have a primer on marital relations so we aren't ignorant, you have to be gentle with me."

"I promise I will, the first time, and perhaps the second." His eyes smoldered and he ran his knuckle along her cheek. "But the third, beware my lady, all my animal instincts will surge to the fore and you'll be ravaged from limb to limb."

"I wouldn't want it any other way. And soon we'll have deep understanding of one another, along with our vibrant attraction—a perfect match." She retreated to the other side of the desk, far from his tantalizing touch. She smoothed down her flowered dimity round gown.

"I must admit, you are correct, my naughty little minx." He leaned over the desk, his gaze intense. "I understand we both have feral natures, that only we can temper and satisfy together."

She shivered and retreated another step. "True. But I'll never forgive you for turning me into a muddle-headed bride-to-be. It must be something like rushing adrenaline that is mucking up my mind and sense of self." She took a long, cleansing breath. "I'll soon be back to normal then it is *you* who must be on guard, my Viscount of Merther."

****

Griffin stood before the communion table in the cob-walled, thatch-roofed chapel on his estate. Not the place where his parents had met their accidental demise, but the smaller, mustier one with the ordinary hard benches and stained walls white-washed with lime. Here his tenants usually worshiped.

The parishioners sat at the ready while the vicar intoned his sermon, then the sacred and binding wedding ceremony.

Miss Pencavel looked gorgeous in her cream-colored gown with lace trim. They recited their oaths and he slipped the ring on her finger. He melted when she smiled at him, glad he'd had no urge to run from the chapel and hide in the sheep shed before the final *I Dos*.

"I present to you, Lord and Lady Lambrick, Viscount and Viscountess of Merther," the vicar announced.

The people stood, applauding. Beribboned and flowered hats bobbed as chatter began. Mrs. Loveday, dressed in somber widow's weeds, wailed and blew her nose loudly.

"Well, my dear, for better or worse. We belong to one another." He linked his arm with his new bride's and they walked down the aisle and out into the crisp autumn air.

His wife stared up at him with flashing blue eyes. She caressed his sleeve. "Let us pray for far more 'better' than 'worse', though I will give you a run for your money, sir."

People started to throw grains of wheat for fertility. Miss Trefoile pelted hers at the new viscountess's head as her father cheered her on. Her mother sobbed hysterically on Trefoile's shoulder.

"Who is that demented red-haired person? Red hair should be dyed, as it's not popular." Melwyn asked, ducking the onslaught. "The sheriff is here somewhere. He needs to be apprised of this."

"Never mind, but watch your back on occasion." Griffin glared at the family as he brushed grains from his frock coat lapels. "If you visit the Trefoiles, as any good lady of the manor should, don't accept anything to eat or drink."

"Is that one of your conquests?" she asked him slyly. "A heart you've broken, you lascivious cad?"

"Hardly, and she always ran a poor second to you." He hugged Melwyn close and kissed her cheek. His body heated with passion and, more importantly, love for her. "Everyone pales before you, my dearest."

"I'll say the same about you, sir." She laughed, eyeing his legs in their white silk stockings. His polished shoes with silver buckles. "I've been keeping busy at the guest cottage. Together with my abigail, we've sewn you a crimson toga to wear in Italy."

"Will I be required to feed Christians to the lions?" He helped her into the carriage festooned with pink camellias and yellow daffodils, the scent heady.

"Only if they're bad Christians. Start with that family of slingers back there." She arranged her gossamer skirts around her shapely legs, her white silk slippers peeking out from the hem. "Some people don't know how to behave in public."

"Your wish is my command. I've even given up my illicit activities for you, so see how you've reformed me." He sat beside her and took her delicately gloved hand in his larger gloved hand. The driver started the team of white horses sporting ostrich feathers down the path.

His tenants gathered to wish him well, tossing flowers, and more grain. Some of the women grappled for the grain, complaining they could make much needed bread with it.

The open carriage rambled down the path past pungent hedgerows and beeches with fiery orange leaves.

Griffin draped a cream-colored shawl over her shoulders. "I can't wait for night to fall, for us to be alone. Are you nervous, my dear?"

"You promised to be gentle." She patted his thigh, her cheeks flushing, and he desired her all the more. "I'm not much on shyness, but on this I must prevail."

"Tender as a lamb, you may be assured. Don't hesitate to partake of the mead to relax you." Griffin held fast to her hand, satisfied to at last have found the ideal woman for his erratic nature; a woman who craved adventure as well as he.

****

"Don't fret, my anxious Clowie, I'm still the same spitfire mistress you've always loved." Melwyn sprinkled rose petals across the large bed. The wedding had taken place that morning, and now the sun was setting. The revelers had drank their fill and were staggering back to their homes; the higher-born were staying the night in the manor's many guest rooms. "If you hear me scream later, rush in and yell the French have landed."

"That be more like it, m'lady." The abigail laughed, her round face content again. "More 'an one rampart will be breached tonight."

Melwyn had second thoughts about the French, recalling Griffin's brother. And the idea of ramparts being violated made her quiver. She tugged her white dressing gown closer around her.

At a knock on the door, her father entered. "My dear, my dear, it does my heart good to see you married at last." He clasped her upper arms, his half-spectacles nearly sliding off his nose. "And safe from an accident in Pompeii, and a kidnapping. I daresay you've had too many misadventures. I hope you'll be happy. Much happier than your mother and I ever were."

"Papa, you do understand that mother left you, and isn't dead, don't you?" Melwyn met his sad blue eyes. He smelled of sandalwood and home. "She even left the second under-butler."

"But you must understand my delusion. She'll always be dead to me, my dear." He cocked his triangular face, his smile warm.

Aunt Hedra surged in, a jeweled-encrusted bandeau wound around her hair. In her very round, purple round gown, she resembled an exotic Oriental temple. "Oh, dear brother, get a grip on yourself at last. Marry the Widow Whale, or some other idiotic female, and move on with your life."

"Mother is still alive, I've *told* you. I unfortunately had the extreme displeasure of speaking with her in Dover." Melwyn sighed, recalling their frigid discourse; then she smiled indulgently at her father. How much the poor man had suffered. She kissed his cheek. "Petition for a divorce before the King's Bench. Lord Lambrick will assist you with the particulars."

"Waste o' breath; the master won't listen, never does." Clowenna flicked grains of wheat from Melwyn's hair. "That drab Trefoile chit flung that grain with extra vigor, didn't she? With her fat papa guffawing. I almost pushed her down the hill."

"I'm glad you thought of it, but didn't go through with the assault." Melwyn laughed, embracing and shaking her maid from side to side. "We must show some decorum now that I'm a viscountess."

"Has anyone instructed you about the delicacies of the matrimonial bed? That is, the intimate aspects?" Aunt Hedra asked, leaning close as she fingered her quizzing glass that hung from a chain around her throat. Her jewels sparkled in the candlelight.

"Egad, I'll be on my way to retire." Her father's face flushed and he headed for the door. "I spent most of *my* wedding night alone, and my valet was conspicuously absent."

"No, Auntie," Melwyn admitted after her father left, "men write erotic poetry about the act—so I've been told. But women are forbidden such enlightenment. However, I've seen horses mating, and it didn't look at all comfortable for the mare."

"Oh, my child, it's much better for humans. Lord Penpol was the most tender of lovers. Just tell your husband to be patient, and you must be willing to play along with his quirks." Aunt Hedra winked, then laughed. "All right, no more of this talk on your wedding night." She raised up a single stocking. "In the time-honored Cornish tradition, I'm here to whip you into bed."

Clowenna removed a belt from the dresser, her expression jubilant. "As am I, m'lady. An'I cannot wait."

Lord Lambrick entered, looking elegant, freshly shaved, and striking in a red dressing gown. Not quite a toga, but close. He grinned, showing his perfect white teeth. "Should we have a hand-fasting as well? Tie our hands together and jump over a broom?"

"Let them have their fun." Melwyn clasped his warm strong hand and led him over to the four poster bed. Inside, she trembled, beginning to fear what might happen soon. Three glasses of sweet mead eased her jitters somewhat.

"Be good to him, my lady—though I'm not certain the term 'lady' applies." The housekeeper drifted in dressed in black as she had at church, as if she mourned rather than celebrated. "His lordship deserves a loving and dedicated wife." She glared at Melwyn.

"Be at peace, Mrs. Loveday, I will be a superb wife for his lordship." Melwyn kept the part of her not being very obedient to herself. She smiled at Griffin, her heart lifting.

"Indeed, Mrs. Loveday. I promise we will be a volatile but devoted couple." He pressed his housekeeper's shoulder. "Please, go on to bed."

"I'll pray for you, sir." The woman sighed heavily, shook her head, pulled a black veil over her face, and departed the chamber.

"*Commonzee*," Clowenna called. "I must throw me belt at 'ee. Hasn't got all night."

"Get into bed, you two," Aunt Hedra insisted. "Let's do this correctly."

Melwyn swallowed nervously and crawled between the cool sheets. Griffin followed, his weight shifting the mattress, his warmth distracting.

At the last minute, Sir Arthur hobbled in. "Did I miss anything, old beans? Always late to the party, sad to say." He held up a stocking with a tiny pebble in the toe. "I'll try not bonk anyone in the head."

Kenver, Griffin's valet, entered. He smiled at Clowenna, and the maid blushed.

"Fashionably late, ess?" she admonished with a suggestive wink. "Never keep a lady waitin'."

"I had important duties, but couldn't wait to see you again," the valet replied with quiet dignity. "Or to join in this custom on my lord's auspicious night."

With a jingle of panniers, the Duchess of Dumfort glided in. "Here I am, as instructed. What exactly am I to do with this stocking?" She held the item up and wriggled it. "Whip someone? Upon my word, you Cornish are pagans of the first order."

"You'll be fine, your grace. You need to experience new things. All right, everyone ready?" Aunt Hedra raised her stocking where a small diamond nestled in the toe. "I eschew pebbles for stones of value."

Melwyn stiffened in the bed, her body so close to Griffin's heat, the dressing gowns still wrapped around each of them like shields. Her fingers kneaded at the down mattress.

"So sorry about this, my lord." Kenver tossed a belt, which landed in Griffin's lap. "But it is our tradition."

Aunt Hedra's stocking struck Melwyn on the knee. Sir Arthur's grazed Griffin's shoulder. Clowenna threw her belt, after extra-careful aim, and smacked Griffin's chest.

"I don't know if I can do this. The duke would not approve." The duchess put one hand over her eyes and flailed the stocking with the other. The silk floated to the floor just shy of the bed. "I'm certain it's some sort of blasphemy."

"A boy, your first babe will be a boy!" the abigail proclaimed, clapping her hands. "As most of us hit his lordship."

"Bravo, excellent. Well, I give you goodnight. Don't know if I can make the voyage to Italy. Getting too old for it. A shame we found nothing in Pompeii, as you keep insisting." Sir Arthur raised a bushy brow, then bowed out.

"Goodnight, my darlings. Treat my niece well, or you'll hear from me." Aunt Hedra wagged a finger at Griffin. "Hmmm, I'm returning to London as soon as possible, since there's no society here; only sheep and odd stones." She exited, the top of her hair rubbing across the door's lintel.

"Before traveling all the way out to this hinter land, I had no idea England had a West Country. What's it used for?" The duchess followed her aunt.

"If you needs me, I'll be about. Goodnight, m'lady, m'lord." Clowenna sauntered toward the corridor. "Have a hella-ridden time o' it."

"A very successful night, m'lord and m'lady." Kenver bowed, followed the maid, then hesitated. "I'll have my hands full with this one."

The door clicked shut after them.

Melwyn turned to Griffin, her pulse jumping. This was it, tonight she'd be his, and would she regret it later? His dark eyes so full of love assured her otherwise. "Well, at last alone. I pray you'll be gentle with me, sir."

"I will indeed, my Lady Lambrick. I wish to make you exceedingly happy, and never have the urge to scratch off my face as you once threatened." He smiled tenderly, tugged the bed curtains closed, and kissed her as he brushed the dressing gown from her shoulder.

She laughed, and slipped his dressing gown low to admire his toned pectorals. "What if I scratch at your chest instead?" She ran her fingernail over his dark chest hair, wiry and sexy. "We're two tigers enjoying the same bed, my lord. And may it always be so."

"Amen, my love." He kissed her again, slow and yearningly. His fingers caressed down her body, sending shivers all through her. His lips followed his fingers and she groaned with rapture.

Chapter Twenty-One

Melwyn handed the basket of plum pudding, apples, cheese and breads to the woman in plain clothing and apron, whose children clung to her well-worn skirts. She gave each child a toy, a tin drum or rag doll, and sugared almonds. "Have a joyous New Year, Madam. If you require anything else, you only need to ask."

The woman thanked her profusely, and smiled with crinkled eyes when Griffin gave her husband a shank of lamb.

The viscount and viscountess walked arm in arm away from the last tenant's wattle and daub cottage. Smoke from the chimney curled into the chilly air. The bare-branched trees scratched into a grey sky, the pines the only color in the winter woods. The towers of Merther Manor poked up over the tree-line.

Melwyn huddled in her cloak, and against the warmth of her husband. "I'm glad you care so much for your tenants." She laughed after a moment. "And here I was constantly warned of your nefarious character."

"Contented people are loyal—but I do care about my workers." He arched a sardonic eyebrow. "I'm still quite the rogue, as I'd hate to lose all my reputation, but mostly in the bedroom now, with you."

"Well, at least you gave up your more dangerous activities. Do you miss it?" She ran a gloved finger down his arm as she admired his patrician profile. "I don't want you to get bored."

"I've hardly had the chance, given the intimate time I spend with you. And you're never boring, especially after what I've taught you at night." He grasped her hand and quickened his pace; his jackboots swished through the soggy, dead leaves. "Though my smuggling wouldn't be quite the same without Jacca. I hope he's nearly to New South Wales. He promised to write."

"Such a long voyage. The poor man has suffered, after what you told me about his wife. I'd never waste good crockery by throwing it at your head." She leaned into him again. "That harridan makes me seem absolutely angelic."

He laughed. "No, you're still a witch of the first order, and have cast a spell on me."

They entered the woods, where even colder air seemed stalled in the danker shadows. The smell of moldy plants and moss drifted up.

She shivered. "We should have brought mulled ale, to warm us."

"Aren't I the only heat you need, my love?" Griffin chuckled, squeezed her, then kissed her temple under the brim of her bonnet. "I could slip behind a tree here and fire you up with a burning log."

"You are besotted, as well as depraved, sir," she teased as she navigated the muddy path, where ice crystals floated in tiny pools of water. Her heart soared at the perfectness of their relationship. His solicitous toward her was a lovely surprise, and shock.

"I am both, and don't mind either at all." He tightened his arm around her. "We'll soon be off so I may attend Parliament—late as I may be—in town; a London town home is being made ready for my esteemed wife. I daresay I must play the affable host for the *ton*, to reinforce old acquaintances for the future. If the season won't be too arduous for you."

"I think most of my nausea has passed." She rubbed her stomach lovingly, thinking of gurgles and coos, and nappies she wouldn't have to change since they could afford a nurse. "A July baby, I should think. But we can still sail to Pompeii in earliest spring, to uncover my treasure."

"I doubt I could stop you, however, I'll try. Remember, the war continues." His voice grew serious, his fingers on her stiffening. "The Austrians sent another army to defeat the French, and that rapacious Corsican general, in November. Alvinczi and Davidovich prevailed at Bassano, Calliano and Caldiero in Italy. But Buonaparte defeated them at the Battle of Arcole in the middle of the month. Italy will be very treacherous."

She mused on her discovery, the statues, the vases and jewelry. Her shoulders sagged as she stepped over a protruding tree root. "While traveling through a war torn country sounds exciting, and we can pray the war will end before then, I suppose I must be mature and think of you and the baby."

"You're agreeing with me? Your fall in Pompeii must have injured more than your leg." Griffin grinned and winked. "I'll send more trusted men over to catalog everything in the hole, and continue to protect the site."

"*And* as soon as the babe is here, and I'm sure the war will be done," she nudged her gloved knuckles into his side, "we'll travel there ourselves."

He sighed loudly. "I knew I couldn't deter you for long."

Dried twigs crackled under their feet, startling a bird who swept into the air.

"Then we'll visit Greece and Egypt." She beamed up at him. "I'm certain our babe will adore feta and camels."

"Too bad Sir Arthur is too feeble to travel, but he says lecturing at the Royal Society is satisfying for him." Griffin ducked under a low hanging branch.

Maybe the old antiquarian would invite *her* to attend his lectures. "And his visits to Aunt Hedra are amusing him, I imagine. I'm sure they discuss two-decades-past fashions and lament the disuse of wigs."

They left the woods, the weak sun a welcome change, and crossed the lawn toward the mansion. Her skirt hem was soon damp in the rising mist. The air felt heavy with moisture, as if it would soon rain. The grey sky darkened even more. Thunder rolled in the distance.

A figure in black lurked at one of the house's windows, then put a handkerchief to her nose and turned away.

"Will Mrs. Loveday ever stop weeping over our marriage?" Melwyn glared up at the now empty window with its fluttering curtain. The housekeeper was the only thorn in her new life. But she couldn't ask Griffin to dismiss her, given his long affection for the woman. Melwyn's generosity toward the servant gave her a little satisfaction. And she did wish to please her husband, to her own consternation. "Centuries from now she'll haunt this place, intending to knife a ghostly me in my bed, to the pleasure of gaping tourists."

"Don't mind her, my dear. She'll soften when the baby comes. It's your abigail and my valet we need keep an eye on. Their attachment could cause complications. It's difficult when servants wish to marry, but I'd hate to stand in their way." Griffin tugged her into a doorway and pressed her against the door jamb. "However, at this moment, I'd rather concentrate on you, and neither of us needs body servants as we can readily undress one another."

Melwyn's pulse skittered when he leaned in and kissed her lips. She ran her fingers through his thick hair, over his chiseled cheeks, and kissed him back fervently. His muscled chest against her breasts sent tingles of desire throughout her. She'd savor him, her coming child, and her archeological pursuits. "I do like the sound of you undressing me, you debauched and utterly sexy cad. But could we wait until we step inside the scullery, my dearest husband?"

The End

Betrayed Countess

Miss Grey's Shady Lover

Chat with Diane and other Books We Love authors in the Books We Love Online Book Club: https://www.facebook.com/groups/153 824114796417/

About the Author:

Diane Parkinson (Diane Scott Lewis) writes book reviews for the *Historical Novel Society* and worked at The Wild Rose Press from 2007 to 2010 as a historical editor. She has two books published by Books We Love. *Betrayed Countess* (formally published as *The False Light*); and the erotica novel, *Miss Grey's Shady Lover.* Set in the eighteenth century as well, this short novella is a parody of *Fifty Shades of Grey.*

For further information about the author, visit her website:
http://www.dianescottlewis.org

Note from the Publisher

http://bookswelove.com

We hope you have enjoyed your reading experience. Books We Love and the author would very much appreciate you returning to the online retailer where you purchased this book and leaving a review. *Happy Reading Jamie and Jude*

Books We Love publishes top quality ebooks. We have fabulous authors with mystery, romance, suspense, thrillers, fantasy, young adult, science fiction, western and historical ebooks. We have contests that are easy to enter and your chances of winning are great. We also have free reads available on our website. If you prefer your books on the spicier side visit our Spice site

http://spicewelove.com

DISCARD

Made in the USA
Lexington, KY
25 November 2013